Terror Under the Lupin Moon

Book One of the Michigan Macabre Mysteries

By Michele Roger and M. M. Genet

Terror Under the Lupin Moon by Michele Roger and M.
M. Genet
Copyright 2022 All Rights Reserved
Cover Design by Converted Books
Published by Converted Books

Other Books by Michele Roger
Eternal Kingdom: A Vampire Story
The Harpist
Huggy Muggy Do! (as Michele Roger-
Beresford, with Finnegan Dudley)

Other Books by M. M. Genet
The Harpist
Agent for the Orchestra
The Clever Courtesan
Alice and the Masquerade

Dedication:

To the real Dogman, wherever you are…

Chapter 1

Lori ran through the list in her head. Glancing at the passenger seat, she confirmed the cloth bag and the small, hand drawn map with a red circle drawn around the area where she'd found a bumper crop of porcini mushrooms the year before, her hiking boots, an extra wool sweater to change into and a thermos of coffee to drink on the trip back. Parking on the side of the road, she laced up her boots and pulled a knitted hat over her head.

"Nobody has porcinis," she said in a mocking, male voice. "I'll show you, Chef Alex," she said to herself. "Tonight, the Lupin Moon's special will be Porcini Burgundy and you'll have me to thank. Executive Chef position, here I come," she added, hopefully.

Lori took out her phone. "Gourmet dinner headed our way tonight!" she texted her roommate, Amber. She slid her phone in her coat pocket and hopped out of her small SUV. The air was cool and the trees were bursting with fall colors. The smell of pine and decaying vegetation were pungent in the air. Her warm breath collided with the autumn breeze and steam tumbled from her lips. It was the beginning of November in northern Michigan. "Perfect," she thought.

Her AirPods securely jammed into her ears, Iggy Pop and the Stooges blared "Search and Destroy." Dried leaves crunched under her feet as she looked for the familiar rise of the trail. Drenched ferns and pine needles cushioned each step as she pushed towards the clearing. Her hopes rose when she noticed several dead trees with moss growing on their southern edges. The prime elements for porcinis were all there. Damp, cool weather was the perfect condition for propagating fungi.

Taking out the map, she calculated just another quarter mile and she would be close to the location of last year's treasure location. Her mind drifted to the last conversation she'd had with her employer. "We have to find our edge and push it as far as we can go if we're going to make it in this market," Chef Alex said.

"Everyone is doing farm to table," Lori had argued. "I say wild game and foraging will set us apart. Any idiot can serve venison chili. We need to showcase how great the simplest of local ingredients can be with a bit of culinary knowhow."

Chef Alex raised an eyebrow and looked skeptical. "Prove it."

"I *will* prove it and you'll have no choice but to promote me to executive chef," Lori added.

She thought of herself in a kitchen all her own and under her command. Her focus on the earth around her sharpened. This was her chance to shine and she was going to take it.

As her step quickened, her sharp eyes searched the forest floor. Looking for mushrooms in the wild was like trying to find a raven on a moonless night. Porcini mushrooms grew below oak trees.

She scanned the leaves of the trees above her. Something flashed with color, making her stop to take notice. She stood still and listened. She narrowed her eyes at the manmade pink hue in a world surrounded in earthiness.

A sapling nearly her height was weighed down with something. As she walked closer, Lori's heart sank. There was a pink woven nylon pet collar with silver tags engraved with the word "Hobbes" on the front.

She flipped the tag over. No phone number or address. The irresponsible owner could have at least had their phone number included on it. So many pets from town ventured out and rarely came back after entering the woods. Packs of coyotes were prevalent even in areas so close to town. They were scavengers but they would also take down anything smaller than themselves when the pack was running together. Still, it was strange the collar was so high up in a small tree. A cat or small dog couldn't have leaped high enough to land in a sapling's branches unless something larger...

Her thoughts were interrupted by a strange sensation of floating; no flying. Was it flying? Her brain struggled to make sense of it. She was moving way too fast for her own feet to carry her. Speaking of her feet, why weren't they touching the ground? Her head swam at the disorientation of her situation.

She had gone from flying to tumbling. Her shoulder collided with the ground, followed by her hip and elbow. There might had been a cracking sound but she could not decipher whether it was the crunch of dead leaves or that of her own bones. The burnt umber of maple leaves blurred as her body twisted. She was lying on the ground facing up towards the sky. What was happening?

Another sensation blocked out all others. Pain. On the ground, she writhed in pain. She wanted to vomit. She wanted to scream. It was happening so fast. Her logical mind reached out. What was it? Snarling and howling flooded her ears. Something was tearing away her clothes, her boots, her skin. In reply, she listened to her own pitiful cries. The mud beneath her body was cold. She was growing colder. There was a conflict of opposites fighting for her attention. The frozen air around her threatened to take her senses completely while something hot and thick flowed out and away from her core. She was bleeding.

Her plea for help was answered by a sound that made her want to run or crawl away. The sound was something from her nightmares. She heard the ripping and tearing and cracking of bones. There was a distant idea in a forbidden corner of her mind that knew they were her bones being broken, and her tendons being peeled away from her muscles, but it was all so far away. She wanted to fight back if only she could locate her attacker. The day was growing dark. The void of oblivion opened at her feet. She welcomed it. Her fleeting thoughts were clear. A monster was eating her alive.

Her blood rapidly soaked into the forest floor. Would she be more delicious with the mushrooms, she wondered? It was a morbid thought that made her laugh. At least she conceived the idea of laughter. Whether there was air left in her lungs in which to laugh remained a mystery to her. Maybe she should suggest a mushroom pairing like she would for customers at the Lupin Moon. She tried to say something but her throat would not work. In fact, it was no longer attached to her body. Those were the last of Lori's dying thoughts before the thing holding her to the forest floor plunged its teeth into her chest and feasted on her beating heart.

Chapter 2

Amanda Burton streamed her audio book and repeated the mantra aloud, "I am an adult. I am under no obligation to remain in any situation that makes me feel uncomfortable. I love my family but as an adult, I am free to leave at any time that I feel overwhelmed." She felt her pulse quicken as she turned off of the interstate and on to the side road that lead to her small, Michigan hometown. She paused the book and spoke aloud. "It's just one long weekend, Amanda. Just help mom get things set up and then it's back to civilization. You've got this." She practiced her calming, belly breathing.

Driving through town, she noticed improvements since she had been here three years ago. The Methodist Church had a new steeple after a freak June ice storm had taken out the last one. The shops along Main Street had been freshly painted and decorated with large pots of flowers. Backpackers were coming out of the pastie shop. To her surprise, things had improved while Amanda had been away. She turned into a long, blacktop driveway to what had once been merely the town library.

The antique bell that remained from the building's many incarnations rang as she walked through the front door. Amanda stepped over a bleary eyed ginger cat. "Hello Henri," she said in passing.

It was only polite to acknowledge the cat, after all.

"Bonjour," the cat seemed to say as he opened one eye wide and yawned. Amanda rounded the corner of the living room to the kitchen. She stared at her mother sitting half-asleep at the butcher block table. A swell of mixed feelings bubbled to the surface. She felt polar opposite emotions of love and hate and envy and loathing inspired by a complicated mother/daughter relationship.

Amanda had to admit it was impossible not to feel in awe of the elder woman before her. Victoria Burton had been known for breaking young men's hearts in her youth. She became a teacher and later the town's school principal. In retirement, she had become the town historian and archivist. Nevertheless, what Victoria Burton was most famous for were her enchanted baked goods. Lovesick people of all ages would to drive across the country to purchase one of her cakes or a dozen of her cookies 'guaranteed to win the heart of their intended. 'A thought tugged at Amanda's heart. Even with all that magic, Amanda suppressed a wave of tears, her mother was running out of time.

The brass, antique bell chimed again from over the door. Amanda jumped as she poured herself a hot cup of coffee. She peeked around the kitchen door.

"Mrs. B?" Sheriff Ashton called out as he poked his head inside.

Victoria struggled to wake and got up from the kitchen table. "In the kitchen, Sheriff!" She gasped and let out a small scream at the sight of Amanda.

"Mrs. B? What's wrong?" Ashton shouted as he heard Victoria.

"Mom, it's just me!" Amanda explained. "I didn't want to wake you."

Sheriff Ashton burst through the kitchen door. Seeing Victoria startled, he put his body between her and the other woman in the kitchen.

"Sit down, Mrs. B," Ashton said to Victoria as he looked at Amanda with curiosity and alarm.

"Sheriff Ashton Leeming, this is my daughter Amanda," Victoria said, with a bit of pride and relief.

"Sheriff Leeming," Amanda nodded and scowled at the officer. She raised her coffee cup in his general direction.

"Just Ashton, please, Ms. Burton," the Sheriff said.

"Then just call me Amanda," she countered.

"Amanda," the Sheriff agreed.

Victoria squinted at her daughter disapprovingly as she offered the Sheriff a chair. Over her shoulder, she glared at her daughter's coffee cup as Amanda raised it to her lips and took another sip. Amanda gasped and nearly dropped the cup on the floor.

"Mother!" Amanda shouted.

Victoria turned to Ashton and shrugged. "Maybe coffee isn't hot in Chicago. I keep telling her she's been away too long."

Ashton shifted uncomfortably in his chair. He watched Amanda angrily try to soak up the coffee from her shirt front with a tea towel.

"So, what brings you to town Amanda? Are you here visiting your mom?"

"Yep," Amanda replied. She fumbled with the mouse of Victoria's computer on the kitchen counter; trying to send a clear message that her part of the conversation was over.

Ashton cleared his throat. "That's nice. Got any plans?"

Victoria smiled. "My daughter is here to help me sort out my final affairs," she said plainly. "Doc says it's time to get things in order."

Ashton blanched but he recovered saying, "I don't believe a word of it. You're the prettiest and healthiest gal in town."

Amanda rolled her eyes as she carried her cup to the sink with her sweater pulled over her hand like an oven glove. She groaned as she waited for the out-of-date internet connection to crawl its way towards a connection.

Amanda directed her frustration towards Ashton. "Sheriff are you part of the welcoming committee here in Iron River or did you need something," she snapped.

Ashton stared into Amanda's dazzling green eyes and found himself holding his breath at the sight of her striking red hair. "As a matter of fact," he said after remembering to take a breath, "I wondered if Victoria here was up for a ride? Seems we have a crime scene just west of the trailhead. Jimmy says it's a hell of a sight. Your mother knows this town and these woods better than anyone I know. I could use an expert eye and probably some historical records when we come back."

Victoria patted the man's hands. "Ashton, my darling boy, you sure know how to tempt a woman," she teased. "Regretfully, I must decline. I'm far too tired today. Amanda will go with you, though. She may be rusty but she grew up running through those forests as a child. I taught her everything she knows."

"No. I don't think so." Amanda laughed, her mood lightening.

"But I *do* think so," Victoria insisted. "I'm not able to assist Ashton, so I need you to go in my place. Your teenage years were just filled climbing out your window and doing only the gods know what. You probably know the area even better than I do."

Amanda smiled politely and then shooed Ashton into the living room. "Let me just have a little chat with my mom real quick. I'll be right out."

Ashton ducked out of the kitchen as Victoria lingered, her eyes following him as he left the kitchen. She smiled at Amanda, then lowered her voice and spoke in a conspiratorial tone. "That sheriff is lovely to talk with, but it's at least an equal pleasure to watch him leave the room. Don't you think?"

"Mother!" Shocked, Amanda took her mother's arm and hurried them to the opposite side of the kitchen near the hearth.

"Are you crazy?" Amanda whispered.

Victoria waved her hand in the air and the kitchen door closed as if by itself. "Now," said the older woman. "We have a bit more privacy."

"I came here to help you get things in order and make sure that you were comfortable. Do you get it? This family reunion was brought to you by the big C. I'm sorry but that's the reality of the situation," Amanda said. "You can cast spells on my coffee cups until I get third degree burns but I'm not falling for your matchmaking spells. You can just call it off right now with Sheriff Charming out there." She started pacing. "And what the hell are you doing going to crime scenes? You should be resting!"

"Are you finished, dear?" Victoria asked calmly, her expression gentle.

Amanda took a deep breath and thought about her answer. "Yes."

"Good. Now, you listen to me. You know how things run up here. Jack is the weekly postman and also my plumber. I was the school principal and also the town historian and librarian. That was a perk you didn't mind so much as a kid."

Amanda rolled her eyes. "And now you're Iron River's octogenarian private investigator?"

Victoria sat down in a chair by the kitchen hearth. "I'm seventy-two," Victoria lied.

"Then you've been seventy-two for over eight years," Amanda quipped.

Sparks dripped from Victoria's fingers but Amanda didn't feel the sting. Her mother tried. Instead, Victoria argued, "Ashton has only been here a year. He came up here from Detroit to start a new life and he's doing marvelously. He just needs a bit of help when it comes to the nature side of things. He's used to fighting crime in the city, not identifying animals tracks in the woods. I'm not asking you to do this."

"Good," said Amanda firmly.

"Your hometown of Iron River is asking."

Amanda sighed and ran her fingers through her hair.

"It's your civic duty."

A snort came from the other side of the door and Amanda felt her blood boil at both of them. Leave it to law enforcement to listen in on a conversation, of course better that than actually seeing what her mother was capable of doing.

Her mother continued, "You grew up here. Goodness knows it took this entire village to raise a hellion like you. Now that you've returned, it's time to give back to that community."

"I don't want to give back to the community. I want to make sure you have everything you need and leave. And for the record, I'm not 'back'. I'm visiting."

Victoria stared at her daughter blankly. Amanda gripped the edges of the worn wood counter and counted silently in her head. She tried to remember the advice from her audio book but she was too angry.

"You're not going to let this go, are you?" Amanda asked, defeated.

"If I have to stand on this very table singing 'The National Anthem' followed by 'We Shall Overcome,' I will," Victoria answered, raising a wicked eyebrow.

Amanda gathered her patience. She stormed out of the kitchen door, hitting Ashton on the side of the head with it.

He cursed.

"That's what you get for eavesdropping," Amanda said. "Let's go!"

Chapter 3

Looking at the roof, seats, and dash of the Sheriff's Bronco, Amanda remarked, "New patrol car isn't in the budget eh? I think the last sheriff was driving around in this same piece of crap when I was twelve."

Ashton shrugged. "Old is gold. It's got to be a pretty tough vehicle to handle U.P. Michigan winters."

"You could probably auction this thing off to a museum and with the money you'd make, get yourself a pretty sweet new SUV."

Ashton sighed. "You know," he said. "You could be a little kinder. You may hate this small town, but some of us call it home. We might even, dare I say, like it. And while I'm on the subject of kindness…," Ashton turned left at the one street light in the center of town and headed towards the interstate. "You could be a whole lot nicer to your mother. That woman has welcomed me into this community since the first day I arrived in town. She's been the closest thing to family I've had in a real long time. Quite frankly, the way you talk to her pisses me off."

"Why Sheriff, a cuss word! Who knew you had in in you? Hmm." Amanda smirked. "Mom brings you home baked things, right? Just like your mom used to make?"

"My mother's idea of cooking was a TV dinner. And yes, your very sweet mother bakes cookies and things for me. Since when is that a crime?" Ashton eyed Amanda warily as he slowed the Bronco down to turn on to a side road. "She's the sweetest woman I've ever met."

"I suggest you cease and desist that habit immediately, officer," said Amanda, mockingly. "It may not be a crime, but it's definitely not in your best interest. I'm telling you this for your own good."

"And why would I hurt her feelings by refusing her? If you hadn't noticed, which I doubt you have, she's getting weaker. And besides, I work out. A cookie here and there isn't going to kill me."

Amanda's temper flared. She had, in fact noticed that the Sheriff worked out. Did he think she was blind? And yes, she had noticed that the cancer was taking its toll on Victoria. Two lectures in the span of an hour, she thought to herself. Who the hell was this guy?

"Well, Sheriff, my mother is not only the town's retired principal, librarian, and historian, she's also the local witch."

Ashton shook his head. "I don't believe in stuff like that. Your mother? She couldn't conjure water off a duck's back."

Amanda laughed out loud. "She's totally bewitched you!" Amanda shook her head. "Suit yourself. But she's famous for casting love spells into cakes and cookies. Don't blame me if one night you find yourself in her garden, trimming the hedges wearing nothing but your gun belt and cowboy boots."

"Your mother is nearly eighty! I don't know but I find that very hard to believe. There's no need to make things up," Ashton argued. "That must be some crazy mother-daughter thing you've got going on."

A delicious smile spread across Amanda's face. "Ever see a bunch of cars in the driveway at mom's? They're not gathering for their book club, Ashton."

Ashton looked at Amanda suspiciously. "Recipe swap. They all said they get together for their monthly recipe swap. I think it's adorable."

"Is that what they're calling it now? Isn't it odd that they only share their "recipes" under the full moon? Oh, and if you hear giggling, that's mom and her friends in the coven as they drink champagne and watch you do their bidding under their spell."

Amanda watched the color drain from Ashton's face. He turned onto the two track road. As they slowly bounced and swayed in the cab of the truck, Ashton glanced sideways at Amanda. Strobes of blue and red lights reflected off the dash. He parked the Bronco and stopped. He stared incredulously at Amanda.

"Giggling huh?"

"Sheriff, my mother has cancer. She isn't dead. She loves men. She always has. You're the hottest thing under fifty in this town."

He gave her a sideways look of uncertainty, then stiffened at the sound of his own name.

"Hey Ashton," Jimmy called out, distracting Ashton from the conversation. "Sorry to call you out here but I think this is beyond the resources of the DNR." Jimmy stopped to watch as Amanda jumped down from the Bronco. "Amanda? Amanda Burton? Well, look what the cat dragged in. When did you get into town?"

"Just helping out for a minute."

Jimmy shot Ashton a skeptical look that suggested Amanda was with Ashton for more than a crime scene.

"Well, I hope neither of you had lunch. Follow me," said Jimmy.

Amanda's boot landed on dry leaves as she hopped down from Ashton's Bronco. In that instant, a thousand voices called to her in shrieks and whispers. *'Go back, dear sister. There is nothing here but death,'* said some. Other, louder, more malevolent spirits tugged at her with their taunting. *'Come! Come and see what the master has done. He has returned and resumes his curse upon those who cross his path. Come! Come and see his beautiful, cruelty.'*

Ashton looked at Amanda who had stopped, standing frozen at the side of his truck. "You don't have to do this, Amanda," he said, holding his palm upward to wards her. "Stay here. I'll be right back."

Amanda had not heard voices since she was a child. Her heart pounded in her chest. She remembered how naturally the spirits came to her so long ago. She wanted to listen to them and yet, she wanted to stay in the safety of the truck. Her logical mind argued as it replayed the hours of therapy she'd attended since she'd moved to Chicago.

She'd paid good money for that therapy in which she had concluded that the voices were not real. Neither were the warnings nor the invitations she heard calling to her. Instead, she told her self, the only thing talking was fear. Amanda swallowed hard, slammed the Bronco door and headed out in Ashton's direction.

She clenched her fists and her jaws as she made her way to the crime scene. She saw Jimmy first and took a deep breath. Stepping over yellow tape, Amanda saw the severed limb first. Ashton looked up and followed her gaze. He walked over to her and the two knelt down for a closer look. He took a pen from his pocket and pushed aside a finger from the hand laying on the ground.

"What's that she was holding?" he asked. With a gloved hand, he pulled the circular object from her the clutched hand and polished fingernails.

"Looks like a dog collar," Amanda observed. She read the engraving on the shining side of the tag. "Hobbes. Maybe a cat, although it would be pretty big. I don't suppose we know anyone who's keeping a cougar as a pet around here, do we?"

Jimmy shook his head. "Not that I know of but I'll check the exotic licenses back at the office."

Ashton pulled a small bag from his jacket pocket and carefully dropped the collar inside.

Jimmy cleared his throat and looked at Ashton and Amanda uneasily. "The rest of her is over here, a bit farther off the trail."

Ashton looked at Amanda and took her hand, giving it a squeeze. "You don't have to go see the rest."

Amanda gave him a determined smile. "I'm fine. Really," she lied.

The three walked deeper into the woods, stepping over rotting, fallen trees and ferns. The white pines creaked and moaned as if in warning. While Ashton and Jimmy looked down at the scene, Amanda instinctively scanned the forest for a glimpse of the victim's ghost.

Jimmy sighed. "Sadly, this is what's left of her. Usually, I can identify the animal by bite marks but this is too big for a wolf or a coyote."

"What about a cougar?" Ashton asked. "Amanda, you thought the name might imply a large cat?" He looked up at her. At the sound of her own name, Amanda returned to join the other two.

Jimmy shook his head. "Can't find any paw prints in the surrounding mud. An animal should have left some kind of tracks but we just can't find any. The only print we *did* find is this." Jimmy pulled back a clump of ferns. A thick emulsion of mud and blood held a large boot print. "It's too big to be from the victim's boots."

"Which means someone else was here when whatever it was attacked her," Ashton thought aloud.

"Maybe somebody tried to help her and ended up running off," Amanda suggested.

"Maybe. Let me check the emergency line." Ashton dialed his cell. "Ashton here. Any

911 calls about an animal attack come in this morning?" He waited. "Thanks." He hung up. "No 911 calls reported. If someone did try to help her, you'd think they would have reported it."

Jimmy shrugged. "Maybe it's Dogman," he said laughing.

Amanda joined him in a laugh to break the tension of the cruel gruesomeness of the crime scene.

"Dogman? Who's Dogman?" Ashton looked confused.

"Just an old Michigan urban legend to scare kids into staying out of the woods at night." Amanda said.

"It's actually Ojibwe, I think," said Jimmy. He shot Amanda a look, "And if I recall, the story never kept *you* out of the woods at night."

"Jimmy, can you radio that State Trooper office? We're going to need their forensics team up here to take DNA samples and get a 3D image of that boot print," Ashton asked.

"I called them after I called you. They should be here in about twenty minutes."

"Thanks. I'm going to chase up one idea before I turn this collar we found into them. Let them know I'll drop it by later" Ashton tucked the bagged collar into his coat pocket. "Maybe they can get some prints off of it. I think we'll head back to Victoria's and see if there are any records of this kind of attack reported in the past few years."

"You got it, Sheriff. Nice to see you, Amanda," Jimmy nodded.

"You too, Jimmy," Amanda nodded.

"If you don't mind, Amanda," Ashton said as the two stepped into the Bronco, "I'd like to stop by the station before I take you home. Would that be okay with you?"

"Um. Sure. But do you think it's safe to leave Jimmy out here all alone?" Amanda asked.

"Jimmy knows these woods better than anyone I know. And you heard him, Forensics will be here soon."

"Hmm. Ok," Amanda shrugged. She looked out the passenger window of the Bronco and shuddered.

As they pulled back on to the highway, a crackling came over Ashton's police radio.

"Sheriff? Copy?"

"This is the Sheriff. Copy," Ashton confirmed.

"Deputy Jones here. We just had a gentleman come in here to file a missing person's report. Seems his Sous Chef didn't show up for work today. The gentleman indicated that his chef's roommate said she went out mushroom picking this morning and never came back. Copy."

"Jones, can you take the report there at the station? And text me the address of the missing girl and her roommate? I'll head there now."

"Ten-four, Sheriff."

"Amanda," Ashton asked, "I typically take a female officer with me when I interview and deliver emotional news. Would you mind…"

Amanda cut him off. "You and Victoria are SO going to owe me after this day."

Chapter 4

The skittish, you woman warmed her hands round a large mug of steaming tea as she sat on her couch. Amanda sat in a chair across from Amber, Lori's roommate. Ashton had motioned for her to take a seat while he leaned against the door trying not to add to the tension in the room.

Amber smiled at Amanda. "This tea is good. Thank you. I literally can't boil water." She choked back tears. "Lori did all the cooking."

Ashton took out a notepad from his pocket. "I know hearing the news about her death is difficult but we have to ask you a few questions. Can you do that?"

Amanda watched as the girl clutched her tea and nodded in agreement.

"When were you two last in communication?" Ashton asked.

"Lori sent me a text about eight-thirty this morning, I think, saying that we would eat gourmet tonight. She was part of a chef's group. They forage for wild mushrooms, ramps, that kind of thing. She's always home in time to change and get to her dinner shift."

"Who's her employer?" Ashton asked.

"Chef Alex. He owns the Lupin Moon. When she didn't come home, I called him. I thought maybe he had called her in early or something. He said he hadn't heard from her either. That's when I decided to call a few of our friends. He was going to the station to file the missing person's report." She took another big gulp of tea, holding the cup with trembling hands. Amanda got up from her chair and sat beside her. With tears, Amber added, "Lori never misses a shift. She loves her job."

Ashton sighed. "What about her parents? How can we contact them?"

"They're out of state. Lori hasn't spoken to them in a while."

"We'll still need a number if you have it," Ashton pressed.

Amanda smiled reassuringly. "What the Sheriff means is that by law, he's required to contact her family if they can be reached no matter if they got along or not. Do you have a photo of Lori that we could use?"

Amber set down her tea and flipped through her phone. She turned the screen to Ashton, "Here."

Amanda's heart sank. In the picture was the same knitted hat she'd seen in a sealed evidence bag Jimmy had collected from the scene. In the photo, a young woman, no more than twety-five was wearing it.

"Can you text that picture to this number?" Ashton asked, handing over his card," the Medical Examiner will need a copy."

Amber nodded.

"Before we go, why don't I make you one more cup of tea?" Amanda offered.

"I'd like that. Thank you."

Back in the truck, Ashton and Amanda headed into town. A heavy silence had fallen between the two of them and Ashton finally broke it.

"That was kind of you."

"What was?" Amanda asked.

"I noticed it took twice as long to make the second cup of tea, as apposed to the first. You cast a spell on the last one, didn't you?"

Amanda scoffed. "I told you. I don't believe in all that stuff. That's my mother's territory."

Ashton shot her a sideways glance as the passed Patsy's Pasties.

"Ok. I don't believe in it *unless* it can do some real good. That poor girl was terrified. A little spell to help her sleep could only help."

"Like I said," smirked Ashton, "that was nice of you."

"Yeah, well, don't think too much of me. I haven't cast a spell since I was seventeen. I may have just turned her into a frog."

"I doubt that," Ashton laughed as he pulled into the station. "I have to check on a couple of things. It'll just take a minute."

Amanda shrugged and hopped out of the truck. Inside the station, Ashton and Amanda stared at a glowing computer screen.

"Medical Examiner and the DMV concur with a positive I.D. of Lori Parks. She was originally from Arizona," Ashton read. "I guess that's where her parents live."

"She was beautiful," Amanda remarked, sadly. "And so young." The two stared at the smiling face that matched the case file.

Ashton shivered and turned off the screen. He leaned closer to Amanda to reach past her chair and open a desk drawer. His scent of aftershave, leather from his gun belt and coffee wafted over Amanda. Her pulse quickened as he gave her a quick glance. Their eyes met for just a moment.

Ashton cleared his throat. "It's been a hell of a homecoming for you. Let me get you back to Victoria."

Amanda tried to shake the spark she felt with her quickening pulse. "Well, I'll say one thing. You sure know how to show a girl a good time. Corpses of young women mutilated by animals, distraught college room mates, and an old school forensics lesson are all fine and well. Next time, just take me out for drinks, okay?"

"Deal," grinned Ashton.

"Is the guy who filed the missing persons report still here?" Ashton asked as he made his way past the collection of desks in the crowded station.

"No," Tina answered. "The gentleman filled out the report and said he had to get back to his restaurant."

Ashton walked by the tiny office refrigerator, he opened the door and pulled out a large chocolate chip cookie. Ashton motioned to Amanda to have one. Amanda felt her stomach rumble and reached out only to stop. She recognized that plate anywhere. She laughed.

"Pass. Thanks."

"Are you sure?" Ashton pressed. "Your mom's been baking for me every week since I got here. I rarely have time to eat, but there's always time to grab one of these beauties."

"Has she?" Amanda asked sweetly. "Hmm."

Ashton nodded. "Tina, did Jimmy say if Forensics wrapped up out there? I found a dog collar at the scene but I thought I'd check at Animal Control before I turned it in?"

"Forensics won't be here until tomorrow," Tina sighed. "Jimmy radioed and said that Marquette had a multi-car pile up. Forensics is too tied up to get down here for an animal attack."

Ashton patted his jacket and groaned. He gave Tina a thoughtful nod and took another bite of his cookie.

"I think I'll stop in and see Andy on the way back from dropping off Amanda. Maybe he can give me some direction or info through Animal Control. Oh, and Tina," he said through a mouthful, "I'll need the address of the guy who filed the report, too."

Tina handed Ashton a piece of paper. "Here's where he listed his personal address, but everybody knows Chef Alex practically lives at the Lupin Moon." She leaned in with a large grin. "His maple encrusted coho is to die for. It's on special this week."

Ashton nodded gratefully and headed for the door. "Let's get you home," he said as he held it open for Amanda.

She smirked. "What, no fancy dinner with the chef? Oh right, you spoiled your appetite with my mother's cookies."

As soon as Amanda stepped out onto the sidewalk she stopped dead in her tracks; all snarky comments gone from her head. An electric burning feeling crawled down her spine. She felt Ashton return to her side within seconds.

"Get behind me," she said, sternly.

"What is it?" Ashton asked, concerned but baffled. He looked both ways down the street and saw nothing but a sleepy town on the edge of winter.

"Can't you hear the howling? That's no wolf or coyote. Packs of wild dogs make that sound when they're on the scent of prey," Amanda declared.

"So we have a wild dog problem?" Ashton asked.

"No," Amanda replied, "you have a hunting pack close to town and a dead woman found just at the edge of the tree line."

Ashton looked more carefully at the one or two passing cars and the tree line past town. He listened but he heard nothing but small town life. He put his arm protectively around Amanda. For a split second he thought he heard the faintest sound of growling but he told himself it was all in his head.

"It's been a long day," he said. "You're tired and you've gone above and beyond anything anyone should have seen as a civilian in one day. I'm so sorry. Let's get you home."

They got into the Bronco and Amanda locked the doors.

As Ashton turned on to Main Street, he chided, "I know every mother and daughter relationship has its riffs, but Victoria really is something special. I hope you two can sort it out."

"Is this your way of distracting me from whatever I heard back there? If so, you're terrible at it."

"I'm just saying that your mother has been a real friend since I arrived and she needs you and everyone who cares about her now more than ever. Just offering a little friendly advice."

"Look, I appreciate it," Amanda said sincerely. "Let me try to explain. Victoria is a force of nature. She always gets what she wants. I left this town so that, for once I could have what I want for a change." As she said it, she wondered to herself why on earth she was explaining herself. She'd be gone in a couple days. She owed this guy nothing. Still, she couldn't help herself.

Ashton was quiet. His piercing grey eyes stared back at her from under the brim of his hat. "Well, do you? In Chicago, do you have what you want?"

Images raced across her mind. A handsome publisher, a whirlwind romance, the feeling of a first kiss, the touch of his hand as he left, an empty table, a quiet phone, meetings with the bank, stacks of bills in her office at the bookstore. Amanda repeated to herself she didn't need to explain herself or her life. Nevertheless, Ashton could probably see her answer in her expression on her face.

"I'm maintaining my right to remain silent, Sheriff."

He sighed. "That's fair. Miranda Law is a beautiful thing."

Amanda added. "Just be careful with Victoria. She clearly has plans for you and her specialty is love spells. You know Jimmy? He used to do a paper route just so he could pay mom to keep his parents in love potions. He swears that she kept his folks from getting divorced his senior year of high school."

"That's all very interesting but what does that have to do with me?" Ashton sounded skeptical.

"Her cookies are enchanted, along with her cakes, pies and anything else she might make for you. Every month, when the moon is full, she and her friends from the local coven get together, drink champagne and do a summoning spell. Any men foolish enough to eat their hexed baked goods that month are then summoned, in their sleep to come to them and dance naked in the garden."

Ashton kept his eyes on the road but broke out in a fit of laughter. "You're saying I've given a strip tease without my knowledge?"

"Yes," Amanda insisted. "Or maybe you came and fixed a broken hinge on a cupboard or trimmed the crab apple tree."

"Those sweet elderly women…"

Amanda cut him off again. "Were once wild witches of the north. My mother may be dying of cancer but that's not going to stop her from creating a bit of chaos before she leaves this earth."

"No offense, but I don't believe you. Besides, I think it's you who's afraid of her love spells."

"Suit yourself."

The truck pulled into the gravel drive. Victoria was sitting in a rocker on the porch with Henri the cat. Amanda hopped out and ran to the porch. "What the heck are you doing out here in the cold, Mom? Are you crazy?"

"Do you hear them?" Victoria whispered to Amanda, her eyes wild.

"No natural predator would be calling his pack together in the middle of the day." She gripped Amanda's hands.

"I don't suppose I could look through some of the archives for a few minutes?" Ashton interrupted as he joined the two women.

"Absolutely," Victoria answered, feigning sweetness and calm.

The three of them heard the howling this time. Ashton scanned the forest. He chuckled nervously. "Petersen's dogs must be after rabbits again. I've told him he needs to pen those boys if they can't stick to their farm."

Ashton glanced at Victoria clutching Amanda's hands for dear life. He dug deep for some charm. "Now Victoria, I don't suppose you've made anything delicious here I might have for a snack?"

"Yeah, your giant cookies at the station just didn't fill him up," Amanda added.

As the three made their way into the house and into the kitchen, Amanda opened the refrigerator, "Hey Mom, do we have any champagne?"

"Are we celebrating something, dear?" Victoria asked as she sliced Ashton a piece of blueberry lemon cake and gave it to him on a napkin. Ashton took a bite. Victoria slowly made her way to the library side of the house and answered Amanda, "You know I only keep a bottle for my meetings with the girls!"

Amanda heard Ashton choke on his cake as he followed Victoria into the library.

"What are we looking for?" Victoria asked.

Amanda handed Ashton a glass of water and answered for him, "Dog attacks, wolf and coyote pack feeding or attack instances. Jimmy even thought it might be a cougar or Dogman." She laughed.

"Describe the scene," Victoria asked, serious and thoughtful.

Ashton cleared his throat and answered, "Well, the body of a young woman was found not far off the trail near the north of town. The tearing apart of the body suggests an attack by a very large animal or a pack working together."

"Jimmy couldn't identify it by the tracks?" Victoria asked. "Jimmy's the best tracker in all of the U.P."

"The only print we found was that of a large boot."

"Oh, and we found a bloodied dog collar," Amanda added.

Victoria pulled dusty books from the shelves as Henri rubbed his face on the book cases. Old newspaper clippings crackled as Ashton pulled them from dated wooden drawers.

Amanda turned on her laptop. "What if it's a case of science covered up by hysterical myth?" She tapped on the keys and then read aloud."From Wikipedia:

The first alleged encounter of the Michigan Dogman occurred in 1887 in Wexford County, when two lumberjacks saw a creature which they described as having a man's body and a dog's head.

In 1937 in Paris, Michigan, Robert Fortney was attacked by five wild dogs and said that one of the five walked on two legs. Reports of similar creatures also came from Allegan County in the 1950s, and in Manistee and Cross Village in 1967.

"I'll pull out the crime report books from those years," Victoria said. She stood but had to grab the table to steady herself. Amanda jumped up but Ashton reached Victoria first.

"I think that's enough excitement for one afternoon," he said. "Want me to take you into town to see the Doc?"

Amanda pulled out her phone. "I'm calling 911."

The phone sprang from her hand at the wave of Victoria's index finger. "No one is calling or driving me anywhere. I need a nip of whiskey and to go to bed early, that's all."

"I'll help you," Amanda said.

"Not when I have the hottest man in three counties already at my beck and call. Go get your own man! This one's mine and he's taking me up to my bed," Victoria declared. She put on a good show, but taking a step, her knees buckled from under her. Ashton caught her. Taking him into his arms, he lifted her up and carried her up to her room.

Amanda was staring out the window when Ashton returned. She was clutching a coffee cup but he noticed nothing was in it. He brushed her hair from her shoulder as she watched an autumn storm roll in. "She shouldn't have been out there sitting on the porch waiting for us," Amanda said. "Being out in the cold took too much out of her."

"She's already asleep," he whispered, giving Amanda's shoulder a gentle touch. "I've called Doc and he said he'd check on her tonight on his way home. Is that ok?"

"Yes, but promise me that you won't talk about the case unless she asks. Promise me if you need help you'll ask me. I could stay a couple extra days if it helps with your investigation while I set up hospice. She's getting caught up in this thing and it's too much for her."

"Agreed."

Amanda turned as she choked back tears. "Thanks for getting her upstairs. I think I need to bring her bed down here. I could never carry her like you did."

"Look," Ashton said, his eyes so thoughtful and sincere that Amanda thought her knees might buckle. "Here's my cell. Call me anytime. 24-7. I can be here in ten minutes."

Amanda shook her head. "I can handle things here. You have a murder and an investigation."

"Nobody has decided it's a murder. And you only have one mother. For better or for worse," he said. Taking another slice of cake in a napkin, he turned and smiled. "Then again, your mother might call me." He lifted up the slice of cake and took a bite. "Check your garden before you touch the dial pad."

"You'll be the one wearing nothing but a gun belt." Amanda laughed.

Ashton blushed. "Lucky you," he teased. He brushed away an untamed lock of hair from her face. His grey eyes stared at her and her pulse quickened again like it had at the station.

"Thanks for the help today."

She nodded with a smile.

The sound of howling echoed in the kitchen breaking the spell between them. "Petersen's dog," Ashton reassured her.

"Petersen's farm is west of here. The howling is coming from the North," Amanda said with alarm.

"Lock up everything just in case. I'm going to go take a drive. Doc will be here in a couple of hours."

Terror Under the Lupin Moon

"Be careful."

Chapter 5

Ashton had surveyed the back roads all around Victoria's house and connecting farms and neighborhoods without success. The late autumn sun was setting and he had one more place he thought to check before heading home. The familiar sight of Andy's van gave Ashton a nudge of hope. If anyone knew dogs, bobcats or wolves or whatever the hell attacked at the trail head, Andy would know.

The echo of barking dogs filled the parking lot as Ashton parked his Bronco in the lot. He sneezed as he walked into the office.

"Hey Andy, it's Ashton. Where are you?" he called out.

"Kennels! Back here!"

Ashton made his way to the back of the office and through the double doors to the outer kennels.

He sneezed again. "Hey, Andy. Sorry to bother you. Do you have a minute?"

A greasy, young man looked up from cleaning the cement floor and pulled off his rubber gloves. He laughed as Ashton sneezed again. Ashton was surprised to find someone else at the kennels after closing hours.

"Not a dog person, eh?" the guy said, grinning through a gleaming smile.

"I love dogs," Ashton admitted. "Just can't handle the dander." He looked around the kennel as the stranger watched him with amusement. "Sorry, I thought Andy was working today. I wondered if he could help me out."

"Andy didn't come in yesterday so they called me to fill in. I'm Russel."

Ashton held out his hand to shake Russel's but the man just stared at him blankly. The dogs in the kennels nearest the two of them growled and barked. Ashton instinctively took a step back. Russel never relinquished eye contact with Ashton and he never looked towards the aggressive behavior of the penned animals.

"Right," Ashton said, trying to sound casual. "Well, we found this at a crime scene this morning." He handed Russel the evidence bag with the pink dog collar inside. "I just wondered if, I don't know, you had any idea who it might have belonged to? Maybe some tags were turned in? This one's got a name but no contact number."

"Do they have you chasing down lost pets now, Sheriff?" Russel asked. "Taxpayers' gotta feel like they're getting their money's worth?"

Ashton looked solemn as he felt his temper flare inside his gut. "No, a young woman was killed while hiking. It looks like a large animal attacked her and that collar was also found at the scene. Andy knows every stray cat, working farm dog and neighborhood pet in three counties. I thought he might know where this collar came from."

Russel glanced at the bag and handed it back to Ashton. "There's too much blood for me to read it. Looks like it was a pretty tasty meal." Hearing this, Ashton's stomach flipped. Russel continued, "Besides, like I said, I'm new here. Maybe you should try calling Andy." The man added a comment under his breath.

Ashton sneezed. "What did you say?"

Russel cocked his head to one side as he looked down at the dogs in the kennel near his side. The dogs turned to Ashton and bared their teeth. "I didn't say anything, Sheriff," Russel answered with a sly grin.

Ashton shook his head cooly. "I knew it was a long shot. Thanks for your time."

Russel shouted out as Ashton opened the double doors. "You know, dogs have a good sense about people. If your victim was killed by an animal, maybe she deserved it."

A shiver ran down Ashton's spine as Russel stared at him from the outer kennels. Did he imagine it? In that split second had Russel's face changed? 'Who the hell hired this guy? 'Ashton wondered to himself. There was no need for confrontation and yet Ashton fought the inner urge to unholster his gun, despite his better judgement. Instead, he sneezed and nodded. Double checking that he had the evidence bag securely in his jacket, he waved to Russel and left.

****

Amanda quietly knocked on the bedroom door and peeked in on her mother. Victoria opened her eyes and gave her a smile.

"I was just going to go into the library and read a bit more. Did you need anything? I could make you a cup of tea before I look up a few more articles?" Amanda asked.

"You always did like a good horror story to help you sleep. Or is it the thought of helping a handsome law man that keeps your lamp burning?" Victoria teased.

"Your hallway light is keeping all of the mice away," grumbled another voice.

"I'm sorry?" Amanda asked.

"What was that dear?" Victoria said.

"I don't know. I thought you said something about mice," Amanda laughed at herself. "Maybe I should just go to bed now. I'm starting to hear things." She yawned. "Ok. Just holler if you need anything."

Amanda closed the door.

When Victoria heard Amanda's footsteps grow fainter, she nestled deep into her thick, handmade quilts and whispered to Henri, "It's happening faster than I thought it would. She can hear you now."

Henri the cat nuzzled close to Victoria's neck with desperate affection. "I'm not ready," he whined. "She isn't ready. We've done nothing to prepare her."

"I'm not dead yet, Henri," Victoria encouraged. "We don't have much time, but this case will make or break her as a witch."

******

The next morning, Amanda laced up her Nikes and considered her old trail running route. A slight breeze from the open window rustled the papers on a desk in the library. Images of a dead girl's body, torn apart and drenched in blood flashed through her mind and she shuddered. She decided instead on a run downtown before her mother woke up. Amanda's anxiety was high. There were final plans to be made and neither her nor Victoria wanted to talk about it. A run would help Amanda remain calm, she told herself.

She pulled the door quietly behind her and started off at a medium pace to warm up.

The road sloped down past the Presbyterian Church where young mothers were dropping off their toddlers at the childcare center housed in the basement. A few trucks were arriving in the parking lot to set up the Farmer's Market harvest festival. She rounded the corner past Betsie's Pasties and the Village Grocer. Flashing lights caught her eye coming from the corner of Third and Main. She read the sign above the parking lot filled with police cars and Ashton's Bronco. It read, "The Lupin Moon."

Ashton's Bronco was parked in the front of the restaurant. Amanda's head told her to stay out of it. If she went down to see what was happening, she'd miss her chance to finish her run and call the Hospice nurse before Victoria woke up. She'd never be calm enough to have that serious talk, she told herself sternly. Her heart and curiosity were clearly in charge of her feet because she found herself headed to the crime scene despite the logical argument in her head.

Puffs of her warm breath hit the crisp air and Amanda suddenly felt cold as she ducked under the crime scene tape.

Ashton called her over. She stood next to him and watched the crime scene photographer snap one picture after the next. "Another attack. I guess this takes Chef Alex off of the suspect list."

"And lands him on the list of recent victims," Amanda added, morbidly.

As she looked more closely, her stomach flipped. This time, the carnage wasn't hidden under forest ferns and moss. There were no dry leaves or mud to conceal the bits of flesh torn from his midsection. The victim's blood oozed black from his throat and chest and made pools on the parking lot cement. The sun shown brightly on Alex's grey face, frozen forever in a never ending scream. His eyes were cloudy as the liquid in his eyes had frozen some time in the frigid night. She shivered for a moment as she recognized the same huge bite marks in his neck and chest.

She pointed to the chef's hair. "What's that?"

Ashton took a closer look. "Looks like some kind of animal fur mixed in his head wound." He pulled a bag from his pants pocket and with gloved hands took the sample into evidence.

Amanda cocked her head to one side. "What's that in his shirt pocket?"

Ashton took a closer look and pulled out the yellow scrap of paper. "Some might say you have an eye for this kind of thing, Amanda. Looks like some kind of list maybe?"

"Some might say I just have nice eyes," she joked, trying to make light of the gruesome evidence. Ashton handed her the evidence bag with the paper.

"Bay City Chop House, Celia's Farm to Table, Petosky Wine and Charcuterie," read Amanda. "It's just a list of restaurants in the area." She shrugged. "The restaurant business is cut throat. Maybe he's just writing out a list of competitors." She flipped over the paper. "Actually it's a piece of a ticket," she said. "Look, there are some printed numbers at the top. What kinds of names are these?"

"Bailey. Bad to the Bone. Carson's Curse. Damien. Hex," she read aloud.

Ashton shrugged. "Names of guys in his punk band?," he joked. "I don't think those mean anything. And do you think the restaurant business is so competitive any one of the owners of these places would be capable of murder? I doubt Chef Alex was killed by an animal trained to attack in the middle of town," Ashton said skeptically, his voice harsher than she'd ever heard before.

Amanda raised her hands in surrender. "What do I know? I'm just a bookstore keeper." She handed Ashton the evidence and turned to leave.

The sun was up and Victoria would surely be awake. They had put off the talk about Hospice long enough. A feeling of dread washed over as she looked towards the house on the hill. She stretched and started her slow warm up pace once again.

"Hey, wait," called Ashton. He looked again at the ticket. He caught up to Amanda who had slowed but not stopped her hasty exit. Ashton grabbed her hand before she could set out on her run. "I'm sorry. I appreciate any observations you have. I'm just tired. This thing kept me up all night."

"And here I thought you'd been dancing in the garden and I'd missed it," Amanda hedged trying to avoid the feelings of the day before.

"Do you always do that?" he asked.

"Do what?"

"Make a joke when something's bothering you?"

"You want me to be serious?"

"That would be a nice change," Ashton smiled.

"What could be bothering me? My mom is dying of cancer in a town that will probably have me snowed in before I can arrange for Hospice. Said town has a gastro-cougar on the loose with a taste for killing chefs and all the Sheriff can do is stay up worrying while he eats my mother's spell-drenched lemon cake." She exhaled. "Have I missed anything?"

Ashton wrinkled his nose. "Don't forget that Jimmy thinks it's the Dogman."

Amanda laughed. "Yes, I forgot. The whole town is whispering that all of it's a repeat of the Dogman murders of 1961."

Ashton's smile faded. "Dogman murders? Wait. I thought that was just some urban legend."

"Yes and no." Amanda shrugged. She looked at her watch. "Look, I've got to go. Mom will be looking for me and I never even looked up the number for Hospice. Come up to the house when you're done here. I stayed up last night and pulled out some articles from the murder spree in '61."

Ashton nodded, "You didn't have to do that. Thank you." He nodded. "This case gets weirder and weirder. I appreciate the help." He paused, thoughtfully. "Will it be okay with Victoria?"

Amanda blushed. "Thank my insomnia for the articles. As for Victoria, there's no keeping her away after a second murder nearly at her doorstep." She smiled back and started heading home.

Amanda stretched to prep for a full on run back to the house. She began a slow jog just past the parking lot. Ashton watched her for a moment, her ponytail swinging as she picked up the pace. Then, he turned his attention back to the crime scene.

As Amanda rounded back to Main Street, her pace quickened. Images flooded her mind; the body of a young woman in the woods, a bloodied dog collar, the red and black blood pooled around a dead man's throat, yellowed newspaper clippings and faded reports of rare wolf pack attacks. There weren't enough pieces to put the puzzle together and yet there were too many to dismiss. She stopped at the crosswalk at Third to wait for the traffic to clear. Her deep thoughts were interrupted by the squeal of brakes and barking of dogs.

She looked at her fitness tracker and then raised her head to see what all the commotion was about. She watched Russel as he stared at her from the driver window of his Animal Control truck. She smiled and gave a friendly nod. Russel flashed her a wolfish smile with his perfect, white teeth. Had she imagined it or had he licked his lips hungrily as the light turned green? He laughed as he hit the gas and the dogs in the back of the truck began to howl.

"Creep," Amanda muttered.

Terror Under the Lupin Moon

Chapter 6

"I really have no idea how you can drink coffee at eight o'clock at night and still fall asleep," Victoria chided. Amanda shrugged as she turned the page of a yellowed newspaper. Victoria continued her intense stare at her daughter. She wrung her hands. She cleared her throat, "You know, when I'm gone, someone is going to have to look after this place, not to mention the town."

"Don't forget moi," interjected Henri the cat. "Even great hunters and protectors need love and attention."

Amanda jumped out of her chair at the sound of the voice, knocking over her cup of coffee and spilling the contents all over the floor. In an instant, the hot liquid hovered over the newsprint with a gentle flick of Victoria's wrist. The coffee floated through the air and landed with a small splash back into the cup. While Amanda had grown accustomed to her mother's abilities, she stared wide-eyed at Henri.

"When did the damned cat start talking?" Amanda asked, her chest heaving.

"You can hear him now," Victoria whispered in confirmation. She moved her chair closer to Amanda's and took her daughter's hands in hers. "It's going to happen faster."

"What are you talking about?" Amanda asked wide-eyed.

Victoria closed her eyes for a moment. "We'll have to talk later. Ashton is here." Headlights flashed across the window panes of the library and the two women heard the front door open.

"I picked up Chinese just in case you two hadn't eaten," Ashton announced.

Victoria continued to whisper to Amanda. "You'll be at a disadvantage until you understand what's happening. Stick close to Ashton. I haven't been feeding him protection spells in my chocolate chip cookies for nothing."

"But mother," was all Amanda had time to say before Ashton labored into the room, arms full of carry out. Henri purred and rubbed his head on Ashton's boots, hoping to put himself in good graces in the event any shrimp were to fall to the floor.

Amanda shook her head. "Mom, you're tired. We've been researching in the archives too long and it's making us both a little crazy. I'm going to get us some food. Then, we'll show Ashton what we've found.

Tomorrow, we'll call Alice over at Hospice and everything will be fine. You'll see. It will look completely different in the morning."

A howl from somewhere out in the distance made Victoria look much stronger and braver for a moment. Amanda felt an electricity of magic ripple through the air in the room. Victoria gave a little gasp as she looked up towards the ceiling. She turned her grave gaze back to Amanda. "Yes, you're right. It will look much different in the morning."

Ashton came into the library carrying several white boxes and chopsticks. "Dinner with two beautiful women. I'm the luckiest man." He turned to Amanda. "And I have news. You know that ticket we found in Chef Alex's pocket today?"

"The one with the odd list of names?" Amanda asked.

"Yes, well the State Police M.E. called today. They found the same list of names in the jeans pocket of our first victim."

"I know this should be significant but I can't place it."

"What kinds of names?" Victoria asked.

Ashton pulled out his phone and handed it to Victoria. "Here's the picture the M.E sent."

"Pet names," Victoria declared.

"You think?" Ashton asked. "Could be." You don't think they're nicknames for maybe some poker buddies, gambling debts, that kind of thing?"

"That or Dogman has a funny list of aliases," Victoria noted.

Amanda rolled her eyes at her mother. "There are two conflicting theories tonight." She handed Ashton a stack of papers. "First, there's my very logical theory. In this stack are the filed taxes of each of the restaurants in the area that hold any potential for being competition for the Lupin Moon." Her fingers flipped through the papers and stopped at a particular document. She ran her finger down the page. "These two have taken a serious profit loss since the Lupin Moon opened."

Amanda heard Ashton take a deep breath as he read through the profit and loss statements. "Nice perfume," he said quietly. He cleared his throat and asked, "So you think we have motive driven by financial competition?"

Amanda noticed he asked as he looked away from the paper and in her direction.. When her eyes met his, he took in a sharp breath. "I mean. Money isn't everything. Is it enough to kill not once but twice?"

Ashton summarized. "Amanda, your theory is that someone from one of these two competitors killed to eliminate small business competition. And if Victoria's list name theory is correct, they used trained dogs to take down the head and sous chef?"

Amanda looked down at the paper to break the spell of his glorious eyes. "Seems crazy anywhere else but in this one traffic light town, I can name at least ten dog teams for mushing and hunting. If someone offered enough money, I could see some of those trainers loaning the dogs for a hit," she said.

Ashton took a sip of coffee. "I'm not sure I agree. Once a large breed dog tastes human blood, it typically has to be put down."

Victoria nodded in agreement. "That's true."

"That's mine," Amanda laughed, taking the cup from Ashton. "Let me get you a fresh cup from the kitchen." She walked over and shouted. "Why do they have to put the dog down?"

Ashton cocked his head to one side and looked sadly at Victoria. Amanda returned with a fresh cup of coffee and handed it to Ashton. He took a sip and swallowed hard. "The dogs develop a taste for it."

"What do you mean? They get aggressive?" Amanda asked.

"Blood dear," Victoria clarified. "Dogs allowed to attack and kill humans get a taste for it, particularly human blood. While anyone can turn a blind eye to a dog who likes to go and kill a few chickens every once in a while because they crave the taste, killing a person is a whole other story."

Ashton thought of the strange conversation he had at the Kennels and the aggressive behavior of the dogs. Amanda sneezed and Ashton jumped nearly knocking over the papers. Amanda caught the stack. "Oh, sorry. Thank you," said Ashton. "I'm just a bit distracted tonight. Tired I guess. Um, Victoria, you have a different theory?"

"I do," Victoria said. Amanda noted the spark in her mother's voice. She always sounded a bit giddy when she felt her research was paying off. "We found several articles dating back as far as the 1800s. There's also a handwritten account without a date from an Ojibwe chief." She pushed the papers to the center of the table so Ashton could see. "But you're not getting any closer to these documents with food in your hands," she scolded.

Ashton set his noodles down and picked up the archived statements.. Ashton read aloud, "We have sent many hunters out to track Naq'pote. As our fathers and grandfathers have warned us, the beast awakens on the tenth day of the tenth moon of the tenth autumn. Two children have already been found, their bodies washed ashore in the sands of Gichigami." He turned the page. "Did you two see these drawings?" He passed the illustrations to Amanda.

Amanda shuddered at the sight of the charcoal drawings of the mangled bodies in the sand. "They obviously didn't die in the lake. The water's too cold for bacteria to grow and so bodies in Lake Superior just sink. No one is ever found from boat or swimming accidents," Amanda pointed out. She looked at Ashton. "These Ojibwe children must have been killed in the shallows or on the shore for the bodies to be found."

Ashton stared at her incredulously.

"What?!" Amanda asked.

"You're a little bit scary when you know things like that," Ashton confessed.

"Own a bookstore. I read. I know things," Amanda spat.

Victoria showed Ashton another book with more articles.

He read to the other two, "Christmas 1921, from the Marquette Herald. Two hunters were arrested for drunken behavior after causing a disturbance on their way home from a Christmas Eve meal at Aunt Mary's Tavern. When questioned by the local sheriff the next morning, the two claimed that they and another man were attacked. The assailant is described as a towering figure who resembled a huge wolf walking on two feet. They claimed the 'Dogman 'attacked the third man and dragged him down an alley.''

Amanda stood up. "Hey, this one is from the Herald three days later. Look at the front page."

Ashton stood behind her and read over her shoulder. His body, pressed lightly against hers, made her pulse quicken. His breath, as he read was warm on her neck.

Ashton read, "Dogman Devours Good St. Nick. A shocking discovery awaited Mrs. Ellen Landry, the owner of the White Pine Hotel yesterday when, while taking out the trash behind her establishment, she discovered a bloodied pant leg and boot. Mrs. Landry first thought it was just a piece of a Santa suit left behind or discarded after Christmas festivities. Upon further inspection, she was horrified to find that the pant leg in fact held the remains of a man's human leg, complete with black boot.

"Local children fear the Dogman may have taken Santa Claus as a last meal before returning to the woods. We will have to wait until next year to see if the good boys and girls of Marquette will find presents from the jolly old elf. Police say the victim is identified as James Macky, a local hunter by trade. Police are asking for any information of sightings of an extremely large wolf and ask the public to remain calm."

Ashton stepped away from Amanda and began to pace. He said nothing for two whole passes around the room. Then he concluded, "So those are our two theories," he thought out loud. "A financially disgruntled restaurant owner committed murder via a pack of trained sled dogs or an Ojibwe mythological creature that comes to town every few hundred years is back to feast on humans before the snow falls."

Victoria yawned. "Well, it is the year for it."

Ashton considered. He turned to Amanda. "Your motive for two chefs murdered is sheer corporate competition."

"Yes," Amanda agreed.

"And yours is?" Ashton asked Victoria.

"Chefs are tastier."

Sheriff Ashton and Amanda asked simultaneously, "What?!"

"Well sure," Victoria explained, wrapping her cardigan tighter to her body. "That poor girl's roommate said that your first victim was out foraging. And Chef Alex wouldn't have been the toughest competition in the entire area if his food wasn't delicious. Delicious only comes from knowing your food, tasting it. Dogman could go after anyone in town who tasted like a warmed up pasty and a light beer. But why should he? Upper Michigan has become a foodie destination in the last ten years. Why eat fast food when you can have gourmet?"

Amanda and Ashton stared wildly at Victoria.

"Now," she continued, "I'm going upstairs to get a warmer sweater. There's a draft in here tonight."

"I'll stoke up the fire for you girls before I go," Ashton volunteered.

"You don't have to do that. I'll get the fire going again," Amanda said.

"The fire helps me think," Ashton argued. He picked up a cookie once in the kitchen. Amanda followed him.

"You have better things to do," Amanda persisted. "Don't you have lives to save and robbers to catch and peace to keep?"

"That's what I have a deputy for. Besides, I'm on call but I'm officially off duty. "Ashton smiled and offered her a bite of the chocolate chip monstrosity. She stared at it, unflinching. "What, afraid you might fall in love?" He teased.

"Afraid? I'm not afraid. I'm just," she paused trying to think of the right word.

"You're just..?" Ashton took a step closer. She could smell the leather of his jacket, the vanilla from the cookie, a hint of cologne.

"I'm just...busy," she whispered.

"Uh huh," he answered, his breath on her lips. She drank in his scent.

Everything happened in a moment.

His kiss was warm like a summer day. Her body melted into his arms. A feeling of electricity washed over her. Amanda wasn't sure if it was her mother's spell or that rare, once in a lifetime connection that just happens over a couple of days. As she pulled him closer, letting her kiss match the passion she had been suppressing since she'd met Ashton.

Chapter 7

Ashton pulled himself away from Amanda at the sound of Victoria's approach. He cleared his throat and caught his breath before announcing, "I'm going to pick Jimmy up and check out what happens at closing time at a few of the restaurants on your list. Can I ask you girls a favor?"

Victoria smiled and gave Amanda a wink, "At this point, Sheriff, you're going to have to deputize us."

"It's not a bad idea," Ashton laughed. "In all this, I haven't been able to get a hold of Andy. You know Andy from Animal Control? Do you think you might drop off some of your cookies to him in the morning? He called in sick a few days ago and I'm getting a bit worried about him."

"The creepy guy in the truck?" Amanda asked.

"Andy is the sweetest, most lovely man," Victoria protested.

"I think you mean Russel," Ashton clarified. "He's been hired to fill in while Andy's under the weather. You met him?"

"Not really," Amanda said. "Just saw some creepy with perfect teeth riding around with a bunch of dogs in the Animal Control truck on my run."

"One batch of medicinal cookies coming right up," Victoria declared.

Ashton and Amanda chortled. Amanda put her hand on her mother's shoulder, "I think the regular kind will do in this instance."

Ashton put on his coat and texted something from his phone. He shot Amanda a serious look and she felt her own phone vibrate in her pocket. "No marijuana in the cookies, promise me, Victoria."

Amanda watched as Ashton backed the Bronco out of the driveway. His headlights illuminated the open kitchen through the living room windows. She felt her heart sink a bit at the thought of he and Jimmy sitting all night on a stakeout in the next town over, observing the other restaurant owners and their night time practices. Amanda felt a hand on her shoulder. Victoria gave her one of her reassuring looks.

"I'm heading up to bed," Victoria announced and Henri appeared from nowhere and rubbed his head on her calves.

Amanda forced a smile. "Uh, what about the cookies?"

"I don't do plain cookies," Victoria scowled.

"Right," Amanda said. "Got any cookbooks or recipes laying around?"

Henri jumped up on the counter and meowed. "You're right," Victoria sighed. "But I don't want to," she argued with the feline.

"You don't want to what?" asked Amanda, confused.

Henri hissed at Victoria.

The elderly woman pouted as she stared back at the cat. The cat flicked his tail and then, Amanda heard it as if a radio with static was being dialed into clarity. "It's time to show her," nagged the cat.

Victoria just gave Henri a sour look. She lingered, twiddling her fingers around the necklace that hung to her chest.

"Did I ever mention how creepy it is that you talk to the cat like you can hear him?" Amanda said, trying to ignore the fact that she was sharing the same hallucination. To distract herself, she pulled her phone from her pocket and read Ashton's text.

"Stay clear of Russel. Keep Victoria close. I'll be by to get a full report on Andy later….and another kiss."

Amanda smiled despite herself.

"I do have some recipes," Victoria suddenly answered, "and a whole lot more that

I should pass on to you. Come with me. Bring some wine. No. Bring the whiskey."

"Wait. What? But..I thought you were tired," Amanda asked. "The whiskey?" Victoria only drank whiskey at funerals.

"It's time," Victoria confirmed.

Amanda felt her heart pound as if it might leap from her chest.

The three walked into the living room where Victoria closed the curtains tight, shutting out the bright, November moon. With effort, she pulled back the coffee table and told Amanda to roll up the rug. A small gasp escaped Amanda's lips as she stared down at the floor.

"When the hell did this get here?" Amanda asked.

Victoria stood, winded but determined. "You were always in such a hurry to get out of this house that you never took the time to see the world, literally at your feet."

Amanda stood in awe as her mother knelt down on the floor to open a small golden lock with a pendent that she always wore around her neck. The lock was practically invisible to Amanda's untrained eye. A mural of a raven flying across the full moon had been intricately painted on the wooden planks and within the shining iris of the raven's eye was a tiny golden opening where her mother's pendant acted as a key.

The sound of gears and tumblers clicked under their feet and the trap door popped ever so upward allowing for the elder woman to find the latch and lift it up. The three opened the door to a secret room Amanda had never known. "Bloody hell," Amanda whispered aloud. "I'll be right back," she announced. "I'm going to get that whiskey."

The glow of ambient light filled the living room from a source below. Without a word, Henri and Victoria proceeded down the stairs. Amanda followed a few paces behind, her fear of what Victoria had to say or show her caught in her throat. As she entered the secret room, Amanda laughed lightly. "You sure are full of surprises, Mom."

The floor of the cellar room was made of neatly placed flag stone while the walls were filled with cases and cases of books. A few overstuffed chairs kissed the corners of the room where sconces hung from the upper walls. A smattering of small tables held glass bottles and jars.

Victoria tossed Amanda a book she took from a shelf. "Maybe a bit of light reading?" Victoria suggested.

Amanda read the title and stared back at Victoria, wide eyed. "We have a family Grimoire?"

Victoria rolled her tired eyes, "Of course we do. Your cousin Becky's recipe for oatmeal cookies is in there. Try making those. I'm heading upstairs." She fumbled with the chain at her neck as Henri growled at her sternly. Victoria gave the cat a nod, slipped the chain from her neck and placed it on the table. "Don't forget to lock up when you're done."

"But.." Amanda stammered. "That's it? You're going to bed? I thought we were having a whiskey. And you needed to tell me things. Important things."

"What do you want me to explain, dear? Why did I never tell you about this place? You weren't ready. Now, ready or not, you're the keeper of this place and all the good it can do for this town and the rest of the world." The elder woman gave herself a heavy pour of whiskey in a glass and took a long sip. "My time is done. Don't let me down. If you need help, Henri will help you." Her face was gravely serious and angry and Amanda knew not to argue.

"I'm going to fall into bed," Victoria mused. "The fire extinguisher is under the kitchen sink." She gave Amanda a wink. "You know, in case Aunt Becky's cookies are too much for you."

"Mmhmm," Amanda answered, her mind spinning with a million thoughts. She stopped and wondered, asking, "Mom! Um, if this is our Grimoire, why is there a recipe for plain old, oatmeal cookies?"

"Your cousin Becky was as dull as they come. There wasn't an ounce of magic in her." Victoria sighed. "But we didn't want her to feel left out."

"How uncharacteristically nice of you." Amanda cocked her head. "Mom, seriously," Amanda said quietly, waving her hands at everything in the room. "All this, I mean, I didn't..I mean, I wish..I'm sorry." There was a silence that painfully cut both of them.

"While you're baking, better bring up a few of those books on protection spells. I have the feeling that these murders are much more than just corporate rivalry. If you're going to protect this family and your one shot at love you'd better do some reading. Henri and I will give you a crash course in your birthright bright and early in the morning."

Chapter 8

Amanda ran her fingers along the dusty spines of her mother's secret library books. Her bookshop keeper eye could only guess at the ages and auction value of some of the volumes. She randomly pulled books from the shelf, glanced through its pages and then replaced it gingerly. In the twenty minutes she had slowly scanned the shelves of books, she had counted editions in at least six languages. She rounded a corner and opened another random book.

"How's your Ancient Greek?" Henri asked.

Amanda jumped. "Jesus!" she gasped. "Hearing you speak is going to take some getting used to."

"It wasn't so strange when you were four," the cat retorted.

"I was open to a lot more possibilities in the world when I was four."

The cat shrugged. "Clearly."

A cabinet sat wedged in between the books. Amanda opened it and took out a bottle. "Yarrow," she read aloud.

"A human medicinal for coughs. Your mother always keeps some down here in the event of a viral pneumonia outbreak hitting the town," Henri noted.

"Dragon't blood," Amanda read another label and raised an eyebrow at Henri.

"It's a fancy word for red ink that stains anything it touches."

"What do you use that for?" Amanda asked.

"Your mother is particularly fond of it in love spells. Dragon's blood is strong stuff. If a couple whom she has helped in the past, suddenly start falling apart, it's not good for business."

"So it's a binding thing?"

"More or less," Henri agreed. "It's pretty useful in legal contracts as well."

"She should have been a lawyer," Amanda commented under her breath.

The adjacent bookshelf contained volumes of scientific books on herbalism, botany, crop rotation and medicinal plants. The edge of the shelf caught Amanda's fingertip. "Ouch!" She peered closer at the place where her finger pricked. "What the hell is this? There's a tiny hole in this edge and it's sharp.

"I think one of these is broken." She stuck her bleeding finger in her mouth. "I can't remember the last time I had a tetanus shot. Please tell me I didn't just cut my hand on one hundred year old rust." She peered closely at the edge of the book case. "The edge is different from the other book cases."

Henri hissed while arching his back. "Stay away from there."

Amanda took one step back to get a better vantage point. She stepped closer again and felt with her other hand, looking for a latch or a spring. If she caught the light just right, the bookcase resembled more a door than a bookshelf. "I've seen these in stage props. Come on Henri, haven't you always wanted a secret passageway to somewhere?"

"I do believe we just came from one, or did you forget the trap door in the floor already?" spat the cat. "Besides, all I smell from behind that bookshelf is death."

"Oh don't be so dramatic," said Amanda as she gingerly searched for anything resembling a switch. Her fingertips passed over a smooth, cold piece of something solid that felt like a polished stone or a piece of marble. An announcement filled the small room, making Amanda leap backwards, clutching her chest and searching for a source of the words.

"Nothing is perfect or as it seems," said a calm, disembodied voice.

"Well, that's an understatement," Amanda joked, nervously.

"A guardian would imply that I held this place of confinement is high regard. I do not," replied the voice.

"Place of confinement. Ok, so you're a ghost?" Amanda asked.

"Of sorts."

"You're here against your will?" Amanda asked.

"Yes. Are you here to help us write the words?" whispered and whimpered the ghost.

"Uh, I don't think so? What words?" Amanda knew she would regret asking such a loaded question but she'd never be able to sleep without knowing the answer.

"The words that complete our time here. The ending of our stories. The desperately important truths we have learned but could not pass on before our lives were cut short."

"Cut short how? You were murdered?" Amanda asked in alarm.

"All life is fleeting. All time is too short," said the ghost.

"And the words are what you need to say but never got around to telling anyone?" Amanda was piecing the clues together. "Sounds like regret to me."

"Yes!" thundered the voice that was one and simultaneously a thousand voices in chorus. "Words are part of the human soul. We cannot leave this place until we put those words down on paper, in a song, or passed on in some way to the living, hence releasing them and ourselves. Then and only then can we be on our way to the next place."

Amanda felt a shiver run down her spine. She noticed that Henri was nowhere to be found. She suddenly felt afraid. "The cat is right. This is a closet full of death."

Slowly, Amanda took several steps to the ladder leading to the step up to the living room. She casually took a book from the bookcase closest to the exit. The lights flickered as she placed her foot on the first step.

"Wait!" shouted the voices. "Please help us!"

Amanda's heart leapt into her throat and she climbed the steps as fast she could. She slammed the door and locked it with the key from Victoria's silver chain. Each clink of a lock tumbler made Amanda breath a sigh of relief. She placed both both palms on the floor as the raven's eye stared back at her.

"A whole thirty-five minutes," said Victoria.

Amanda screamed and flipped her body around to see who was talking. "Jesus Christ, Mother! I thought you went to bed!"

Henri licked his paws and purred. "That's a whole salmon filet you owe me. I think I'll have it poached and served with a side of cream, hmm?"

Victoria sighed as she uncrossed her legs and stood up from the sofa. "A filet of salmon but baked. She forgot the whiskey, which she clearly needs after meeting the Weepers. She also left the Grimoire behind. How will she make Aunt Becky's cookies now?"

"To hell with Aunt Becky and your stupid games and to hell with both of you for that matter!" Amanda screamed. She stormed into the kitchen and took the bottle of champagne from the refrigerator.

"That's only for celebrations," Victoria said, biting her lip. She was enjoying this way too much.

The cork exploded and hit the ceiling as Amanda poured a glass with her shaking hands. She shoved the glass into Victoria's hands. Then, Amanda took a long drink directly from the bottle. She gasped and wiped her mouth with her sleeve. With wild eyes, Amanda stared at Victoria, "Celebrate the fact that I'm not running back to Chicago tonight! I should! I mean how much dismemberment, howling monsters and ghost stories can a girl take? Oh and let's not forget you're dying of cancer. Let's add that to the list too. I'm going to bed."

Amanda stormed up to her room, clutching her bottle of champagne.

Victoria and Henri winced as they heard the bedroom door slam. Henri jumped on the counter and rubbed his cheek on Victoria's shoulder. "I'm very surprised she didn't drive away, actually. Ashton must have slipped her a cookie with one of your love spells."

"Oh Amanda knows better than to eat any confectionary within thirty miles of here."

Henri purred, "How did you do it?"

Victoria smiled, "That girl drinks an awful lot of enchanted coffee."

Chapter 9

Amanda woke up to the smell of oatmeal. She lifted her head off of the counter and blinked several times in a morning blur. When her sight cleared, she saw a large cup of coffee and a small, white box tied with string. "What's this, a peace offering?" Amanda yawned.

"No, it's coffee to get you moving and your Aunt Becky's cookie recipe," Victoria retorted, matter of factly.

"I fell asleep down here," Amanda noted, puzzled. "How did you make cookies so quietly?"

Victoria buttoned her winter jacket. "Your Aunt Becky's recipe is on the box. Put on your coat. We promised Ashton we'd check on Andy and I don't want to be late."

"I need to get dressed," Amanda protested.

"You slept in your clothes. Put on your coat and bring your coffee," Victoria insisted. Amanda winced at the stiffness in her neck and the biting chill from her mother's cold shoulder.

The two slipped into Victoria's old, red pickup truck. Amanda started the engine. As she looked for a cup holder for her coffee she squinted at the label on the box. "Mom,"

Amanda asked, "why does this box say it's from Patsy's?"

"That's your aunt's recipe dear."

Amanda stared wide eyed at her mother. "Not a spark of magic in her, eh?"

"I wasn't kidding when I told you," Victoria confirmed. She tried to hold her frosty demeanor in check but the sight of the box did bring a smirk to her face.

Amanda drove with the defroster on full blast to melt the thick layer of frost that blanketed the windshield. The weather was turning from autumn to winter. Soon there would be mountains of snow to worry about. She thought back to the initial promise to herself of only staying the long weekend. She groaned internally, knowing it was a promise to herself that she would surely break.

Andy, the Animal Control deputy lived on Petosky street, just past the elementary school. It took less than five minutes to get to his place from Victoria's house, even with the fresh coating of black ice on Main Street. Amanda turned the steering wheel gingerly as she pulled into Andy's driveway. She exhaled a sigh of relief when she saw that there was a light on in his kitchen.

An immense shadow passed by the kitchen bay window. It was too fast for a human, particularly a sick human, Amanda thought to herself. She looked over at Victoria.

"Mom, I think you should stay here. You get in the driver side. I'll let you know if Andy's up to having company." Amanda felt her stomach twist. She threaded her fingers through the strings on the box of cookies and stepped out of the car. She walked about half way up the path to Andy's house, thought better of it and returned to the truck where she pulled out a tire iron from the rusted old bed. Amanda expected to hear Victoria argue but when she glanced back through the side passenger window to the driver's seat, her mother gave her a nervous nod of approval.

Hands full, Amanda returned up the path and used the tire iron to knock on the door. No answer. She knocked again, this time a little harder. The door eased open without the use of the doorknob. Her heart did a small skip. She noted the lock was broken upon closer inspection. Three steps into Andy's house and the smell hit her like a putrid brick wall. Amanda dropped the cookies to use her hand to pull her coat over her mouth and nose. She called Andy's name frantically; knowing full well it was futile as she took in the disaster that was the remains of his house.

To her left, Amanda saw several dining room chairs were broken in half. To her immediate right, another one of the chairs was puncturing the plaid couch with its splinters. She held her breath and listened for any sign of life before making her way to the kitchen. As she rounded the corner of the small house to the kitchen, she prayed that the horrid stench was from the rotting food that was sprawled out onto the floor, some still mid-tumble from the open refrigerator.

'Maybe he's just been robbed,' Amanda thought to herself. 'The nights are getting below freezing. Maybe Andy went out of town and a couple of squatters did this.' Something told her that robbery was probably too good to be true.

She peered out the kitchen window and checked on Victoria. All seemed peaceful outside. Amanda returned to the dining/living room and noticed that the smell had intensified. Her stomach flipped and water filled her mouth as she wretched. She pinched her nose and tried to breath through her mouth inside her coat to regain control.

She tiptoed, one hand holding her coat to her face while the other brandished the tire iron, ready to strike as she pushed the door open to the first floor bedroom. Her stomach reacted before her brain could process the scene. Blood soaked the old, brown carpet and ran down some of the wood paneled walls. In a dog cage was Andy's naked, battered body. His corpse was bloated, indicating he'd been dead for several days.

Amanda searched for her phone in her pocket. Her fingers trembled as she started to dial 911. Before she hit send, she heard a noise that sent her heart into her throat. There was a creek from somewhere above her head. Clutching the phone, Amanda dropped the tire iron and made a run for the front door. She screamed to Victoria to drive.

"Drive!"

Amanda was running and screaming, the scent of death and rotting human remains permeated her nose and stuck in her throat. She yanked on the handle of the truck in a panic to no avail. Victoria reached over and opened it for her. Before Amanda could get both feet inside the truck, Victoria had thrown it into reverse and was speeding down the driveway in a spray of gravel. The elder woman whipped the truck around and put the car in drive before the poor old vehicle had time to come to a complete stop to change gears. Victoria punched it, skidding her tires on the frozen pavement but never the less gaining traction from the sheer weight in the back assisting the torc of the truck.

Amanda was frantic and screaming about dog cages and something rotting.

Victoria shoved a small candy into Amanda's mouth and told her to stop. The small confection tasted like strawberries. The pictures and scenes in Amanda's head still flew through her mind. As she let the candy melt in her mouth, the images remained but grew more distant, less personal. Her mind started to put things in order without the driving madness of fear.

"Better?" Victoria asked.

Amanda shook her head yes. "Good," Victoria said, "now, spit it out. Hand me your phone," Victoria instructed.

Amanda handed over the phone she'd been clutching. Victoria hit the green button and said, "It's Victoria. Tell Sheriff Ashton that Andy has been found murdered in his house and the assailant is pursuing us. We need back up." She hung up.

'Assailant? Back up?' Amanda thought. Who did her mother think she was? She watched the elder woman dial her phone while speeding down Main Street.

"Louise? Call the girls. We need a protection spell." Victoria looked like she would say more but tossed Amanda the phone instead.

"Answer it."

Ashton was calling. Victoria kept looking in the rearview mirror. Amanda turned around to see a pack of dogs gaining on their tail. Amanda cursed. Then, she answered the phone. Ashton sounded frantic. "Who's after you?"

It all tumbled from Amanda's lips in a jumbled stream. Andy's decomposing corpse was in a dog cage, the house was destroyed, oh, and let's not forget the immense pack of dogs chasing after them. Amanda tried to make sense of it but all she could see was the memory of Andy's blood splattered walls.

"Put me on speaker," he said calmly. She did so. "Victoria, I'm pulling into your driveway right now. I want you to pull right up to your side door and run inside once you get here. I'll pick off whatever's following you." The women heard the loud clank of a shot gun being loaded. "Bank hard as you turn off your street. Don't stop until you reach your door. Understand?"

"Copy that!" Victoria shouted. Amanda stared at her mother incredulously. Victoria smiled. "It's the adrenaline, dear. It's quite a rush."

Chapter 10

They heard shots fired from Ashton's gun. The two women held their breath. Then, the sheriff rushed into the side door and locked it behind them after they were inside. Amanda pulled him to her without hesitation.His kiss was warm and desperate. His arms were sanctuary.

There was a crash somewhere in the house but her mind pushed it away. She didn't want to leave the safety of embrace for just a few seconds longer. "How far behind you was the pack when you pulled in?" Ashton looked concerned, but still held Amanda; unwilling to break his physical connection.

"Sounded like broken glass," Henri's voice broke the silence.

"I think Mom must have dropped something. I'll go check," Amanda reluctantly pulled away and walked into the kitchen. "Mom? You ok?"

"Wait!" Ashton shouted. His gun was drawn. "Look at the cat." Henri's back was arched. His hair was standing up on end and he hissed as he stared at the staircase. Ashton pulled Amanda behind him as he pointed his gun toward the top of the stairs. They slowly made their way into the living room..

Amanda called for Victoria again, frantic that her mother didn't answer.

Ashton took a step and the second floor bannister above him exploded. Pieces of spindles and flooring cascaded like an avalanche. Something huge leaped from the upstairs loft with a roar that shook the dishes in the kitchen.

Ashton's gun fired twice in a sea of fur and claws and teeth and chaos.

"Henri, get away from there!"

"I'm going to Victoria," replied the cat. "You get to the Sheriff's patrol car. Call for help."

A chair sailed past Amanda's head. Ashton went flying through the air next. His gun tumbled into the air and landed somewhere in the debris of the shattered loft banister. Ashton's body hit the stone mantle of the hearth and fell lifelessly to the floor.

"Sweet and delicious, she was..."growled the half dog, half man towering over Amanda. His eyes glowed in the dimly lit room. "You'll be nearly as delicious. Kitchen witches are such a delicacy. Ten years is a long time to wait." The wolf licked his enormous teeth. Drool oozed in thick stalactites as it dripped to the floor.

"The poker in the fireplace," Amanda heard Ashton groan.

Amanda's heart leaped at the sound of his voice and to know he was still alive. The collision with a stone wall might have killed a weaker man.

Her mother's words came back to her. What had she said? Victoria had been feeding Ashton cookies laced with protection spells? In the same instant that the Dogman looked up to see Ashton's struggling body, Amanda sprang to her feet and ran as fast as she could, slipping past the monster's immense hairy arms and protruding claws. She stepped over Ashton to reach the hot poker and felt the tingling sensation again, moving from her feet through her body and into her chest.

Ashton rolled painfully from his side and slowly stood. Amanda brandished the poker like a shield maiden to protect him. "We need back up," he said. He reached for his gun but grabbed air. He cursed. Taking the poker from Amanda he said, "You have to get to my truck and call for help. I'll hold him off here." The creature lunged at them both and Ashton swung the poker, searing the monster's paw. It yelped in pain.

"You can't fight him alone. He'll kill you!" Amanda protested, her eyes frantically searching the ground for Ashton's gun.

"He'll kill everyone in town if we don't get some back up."

The Dogman laughed. "A sheriff who's been eating the witches cake. There's the taste of sweet justice."

Ashton gave Amanda a desperate, quick kiss. "Now go!"

Amanda didn't look back. She raced for the library, wove her way through the long tables and bookcases and fumbled with the lock of the door. It resisted but eventually bent to her will. She yanked the door open with all of her might and ran into the frigid air.

Ashton's truck was close. She kept running. Her heart jumped into her throat as she heard crashing and the sound of breaking glass coming from inside the house.

"Please find your gun, please find your gun," she chanted as she opened the door to the Bronco.

She slammed the door behind her and jammed the locks down with her fist. Amanda fumbled with the CB and pressed a trembling thumb to the large button on the side of the receiver.

"Officer down! Officer down! Requesting help at 2367 Library Lane."

"Who is this?" Jimmy's voice crackled over the radio.

"Jimmy. Thank god. Get over here, quick. You were right. It's the Dogman. You were right," she repeated, choking back tears. "He's inside my house. Ashton's not going to make it long. And my mom," her voice cracked.

She had more to tell him but dropped the CB. A pack of huge, snarling dogs appeared from nowhere. One leapt onto the hood of the Bronco and stared her directly in the eyes, challenging her with his growl. Another placed his enormous paws on the driver's side window and pressed his snout against the glass revealing his teeth as they gnashed at her. A boom came from overhead making Amanda scream. The metal buckled the roof of the old truck. Amanda's heart raced and she fumbled for the keys that Ashton had left somewhere on the floor. As she searched frantically, the Bronco swayed from side to side. The windows fogged from their steamy breath.

How many of them were there? Ashton's words flooded her mind, "Bailey. Bad to the Bone. Carson's Curse. Damien. Hex."

Headlights turned the corner into the drive followed by another car and finally Jimmy's DNR truck.

Mrs. Sidway, a friend and coven member jumped out of the first car. "Bad dogs!" she yelled.

"Run! They'll kill you," Amanda screamed from the collapsing box that was Ashton's Bronco.

Mrs. Sidway was moving so quickly in the dark, it was hard to tell what was happening. First, Amanda saw the dog on the hood of the Bronco paw at his face. He yipped as he fell to the ground. Suddenly Jimmy was helping, too. Amanda saw him in the rear view mirror. He fired his pistol. The truck rocked again. The roof above her was a deafening sound of claws on metal, barking and eventual retreat as Jimmy and Mrs. Sidway worked together.

Jimmy opened the Bronco's side door and Mrs. Sidway opened the driver's side find Amanda crouched on the truck floor. When Amanda looked up, Mrs. Sidway, her elderly, retired second grade teacher was the last person she expected to see.

"Victoria called you!" Amanda surmised.

"I see she wasn't kidding when she said she needed a protection spell. I may not have a gun but I've got this!" Mrs. Sidway held up a super soaker water rifle.

"What is that stuff?" Amanda asked as she began to crawl out of the truck.

"Dog repellent. Usually, I spray it on my roses to keep the neighborhood dogs from doing their business in my yard but when concentrated, I thought it might be effective against a werewolf."

Jimmy ran to the driver's side. "Stay here.I'll call you when we've apprehended the suspect."

Mrs. Sidway shook her head. "Like hell we will. Where are Henri and Victoria?"

"Trapped upstairs, I think," Amanda said. "I don't know. I called out for her but she didn't answer. I heard crashing and screaming and then nothing.

Once Mrs. Sidway saw that Jimmy had entered the house, she offered Amanda a hand and pulled her from the crunched SUV. "Welcome to the coven dear. Take this." The elder woman handed Amanda another water rifle.

"What is it?"

"Wolfsbane tea.It won't kill whatever's in your house, but it will certainly make him uncomfortable enough for the Sheriff to get a good shot at him. Come on."

"But Jimmy said to stay here," Amanda countered, shaken from the dog attack.

"You may live in Chicago, my darling girl, but you're a Michigan woman at heart. Michigan women never do as we're told. And if you think we're going to leave Sheriff Ashton to the well-meaning but incapable skills of Jimmy, you've got another thing coming."

Howling errupted from the woods as they headed for the front door. "The pack was frightened but they won't stay away for long. We'd better hurry."

Inside, Mrs. Sidway stepped over a lamp and the kitchen blender as she entered through the front door.

Jimmy and Ashton were taking turns fighting the wolf, one hitting it with whatever heavy object they could find while the other one searched frantically for Ashton's gun. Amanda came in through the library and arrived to witness the Dogman throw Ashton to the floor, his body landing in a pile of debris.

"Ready? Aim. Fire!" Mrs. Sidway screamed. The two women attacked from opposite sides with their wolfsbane ladened water cannon's.

Dogman screamed and roared in fury as his fur smoked and his clawed fingers feebly attempted to clear the poisonous liquid from his eyes. Amanda slowly eased her way in front of Ashton, never breaking the stream.

"We're going to run out of this stuff quickly, gentlemen."

A pounding and scraping thundered at the back door. Dogman howled. The pack of dogs outside howled in reply.

"I'm out!" Mrs. Sidway yelled.

Jimmy, Ashton, and Amanda stared as together, the woman threw her plastic cannon at the towering wolf in a final act of rebellion. Jimmy scrambled with the mess of broken dishes under his shoes. He lunged at the beast yelling, "No one messes with Mrs. Sidway!!"

Dogman roared as he dug his claws into Jimmy's shoulders. Jimmy screamed. Amanda emptied her cannon, buying Ashton a few seconds to search for his gun. When he couldn't find it, he picked up a fallen lamp. He met Amanda's eyes and gave her a wistful smile.

"It was never your mother's spells," he said as he threw the side table at the beast. "I fell in love with you the minute I saw you." With that said, he turned to help Jimmy, running straight for the towering wolf.

The sound of shattered glass came from the back of the house. The dog pack was loose inside. They were outgunned and outnumbered. *Where's the Cavalry when we need them?* Amanda thought to herself. She tried to think of something, anything that might save them from becoming a werewolf pack feast. "If only there were a spell..;" she said aloud to no one in particular.

Then an idea hit her like a murder of crows, or rather a raven. The raven and the door and the pendent that she still had around her neck. The basement! There had to be something in the secret room that could help. She gripped the chain around her neck. She ran to the front room and shoved aside shards of broken dishes and glasses. The raven's eye stared up at her and a twinge of hope swelled up in Amanda.

She turned the key and slipped down the stairs, pulling the hidden door over her head. Ambient light filled the small room as Amanda frantically ran from bookcase to bookcase reading off the titles, praying for something obvious that might help turn the tide of the upstairs fight. "'Keep Rosemary at Your Garden Gate, How to Hypnotize Your Friends and Influence People, 50 Spells for Success, Dark Magic and Consequences," she read aloud. "Oh come on!"

The ghosts behind the door heard her and began to call out, begging for their turn to tell their story. They banged on the thick door and rattled other-worldly chains. "Unless you have a way to get rid of a werewolf pack, shut up!" Amanda shouted. "You're all too loud. I can't think."

She stopped. You're all. All. As in many. Amanda ran her fingers around the bookcase in search for the dial key that would open the door. "I'll tell your story!," she shouted. "I'll write down every single story and lead to your murders and everything else." She put the key in the lock of the door and turned it. A huge gust of wind rushed past her as she pulled open the door.

"If it takes the rest of my life, I'll help each of you. But you have to help me first......."

Chapter 11

The ghosts of Michigan's long, violent history poured out of the door and flew up from the basement room. They charged into battle with unfathomable speed, passing through floorboards and walls and swiping at the pack of dogs as they joined the chaos.

Mrs. Sidway was wearily chanting an incantation roughly in Ashton's direction as Jimmy lay bleeding in a pile of books and upturned furniture. Debris flew through the air as ghost fought beast with enthusiasm. Amanda laser focused on Ashton through the bedlam.

She caught a glint of light reflected off of Ashton's back pocket. Victoria's voice whispered in Amanda's ear as a recent memory played through her mind like a movie. "That Sheriff is lovely to talk with, but it's an equal pleasure to watch him leave the room."

Amanda froze. Another movie immediately followed the first in her mind. She was a child and she had learned to summon her favorite stuffed animal to her side. She became so accomplished that whenever she was sad or injured or feeling afraid Jake the Snake came floating from her bedroom. Each time she had summoned him, her skin crackled with an electric sensation. As

Victoria's whisper echoed in her ears, Amanda felt that same sensation ripple up her spine and down her arms. There were no spoken words, no waving of wands. Amanda simply wished for that one thing that would make her feel safe. She willed Ashton's gun with all of her might.

As Ashton fought to pull Jimmy's hemorrhaging upper body from the floor, the Dogman pounced on the Sheriff. Ashton groaned at the cracking sound of his own ribs. The Dogman laughed at the sound of the defeated lawman. He stood, towering over every creature in the room. As the ghosts battled the pack of dogs, the alpha dog, the Dogman lifted Ashton up by his shirt like a prize.

In that moment, Amanda ran up and reached into Ashton's left back pocket. As she grabbed the gun, closed her eyes and squeezed the trigger. Ashton dropped to the floor and rolled landing on his back, kicking and scrambling on elbows and heels like a crab to get away. The Dogman reared up and roared. Extending his claws, he raised his massive arms and prepared to disembowel the Sheriff with one swoop. The monster laughed in his moment of glory.

Amanda had been eleven when she had last held a gun. It had been a .22 hunting rifle and nothing like the heavy, cumbersome .357 magnum service revolver that shook her in her trembling hands. A flood of western movies saturated her mind as she pulled back the hammer a second time, this time with determination. She took a deep breath and held it. Her finger squeezed the trigger twice, firing two rounds.

The wolf took two steps backwards from shoulder wounds. Ashton scrambled to Amanda, taking the gun in his experienced hands. He placed his body between Amanda and the beast. Then, he raised his arm and pointed the gun at close range directly at the Dogman.

His aim was true, hitting the beast directly in the heart. In that moment, the dogs caught in the ghostly fray howled and whimpered as if they themselves had been injured. The Dogman fell forward with a deafening crash. It convulsed and contorted slightly before lying still. As the beast exhaled for the last time, the room filled with the putrid smells of rancid meat, vanilla and wet dog. As life left the creature, his body grew smaller and smaller. Wolf hair fell away to human locks on his head. The body grew thin and the face became familiar.

Ashton cocked his head as he examined the strange metamorphosis. Russell's face and perfect teeth stared back at him on the ransacked house floor.

With the monster dead, the pack of dogs whimpered, their tails between their legs. Jimmy moaned as he attempted to move and the dogs ran away in fear. "Oh now they run," moaned Mrs. Sidway.

"Mom!" Amanda called out towards the second floor. She ran to the staircase. As she ascended a few steps, her foot fell through a broken step. She screamed, falling forward. Ashton ran to her and pulled her back to the main floor.

"We'll figure another way," he said, holding her tight to prevent her from trying again.

A tiny, familiar face emerged from the wreckage at the top of the landing.

"Henri," Amanda cried. Tears streamed down her face. She'd never been so happy to see the snarky feline in all of her life.

The poor cat struggled to make his way out from under a shattered lamp and many broken spindles from what was once the railing. He wobbled on shaky paws, nevertheless graceful and he leapt from step to step and finally landed in Amanda's arms. His body trembled as he nuzzled into her hair.

"She's gone," he whispered. "She held that monster off as long she could. You should be proud. She went out fighting. Hospice could never have contained her and you know it."

Amanda broke down and sobbed as rocked Henri in her arms. She looked over to Ashton and the old witch standing beside him and shook her head "no."

Mrs. Sidway nodded but Ashton looked confused. "I'll call Jerry over at the fire dept. I'll have him bring the cherry picker. We'll have Victoria out of there in no time."

"Ok," Amanda whispered. "Thank you."

****

3 weeks later

Ashton came into the kitchen looking for Amanda. He could hear her in the library.

"So we're all set?" Ashton heard her ask to someone on the other end of the call.

"All set. I'll get this over to the buyer and you should see the deposit in full in your bank account by Wednesday."

"Thanks." Amanda smiled and closed the zoom call on her screen. The electricity of Ashton's touch was like magic as he wrapped his arms around her shoulders.

"Are you sure?," he asked, simply.

"I'm sure. And with the money, I can fix all the damage to the house and spruce up the library. Who knows, there might be enough money left over to start a small bookstore in town." She turned and wrapped her arms around him. "The bigger question is, are you ok?"

Firelight from the outside bonfire flickered in the library windows. "I guess I've never been to a witch's wake," Ashton admitted.

"It can be a little overwhelming the first time." Amanda admitted.

"I don't think I've seen that much dancing female flesh in my life." He paused. "Particularly flesh over forty."

Amanda clicked her tongue. "I told them they're going to get frostbite if they dance naked under the moon."

"I think all the alcohol is giving them a false sense of security," Ashton mused.

"Witches 'brew," Amanda smiled as she corrected him. Amanda reluctantly pulled herself from his embrace and headed into the kitchen. "We should probably send out more food to sober them up." She picked up a platter and offered it to Ashton. "This bread and cheese should knock them out."

"You drugged their food?!" Ashton laughed. "You're crazy if you think I'm going out there. I barely escaped with my life last time," Ashton refused.

A familiar voice came from the floor and jumped up on the counter. "You could always make Jimmy do it. It's the second time he's fallen asleep in my chair," Henri complained.

"Why don't you see if Jimmy will do it?" Amanda suggested.

"Sometimes I think that cat's talking to you." Ashton cocked his head to the side. "But I agree, Jimmy needs to work on his riot control skills."

A few minutes later, a sleepy eyed Jimmy walked into the kitchen. "Hey, Jimmy, would you mind popping out and taking this platter to the ladies?"

Jimmy looked out the window at the dancing women. "You know someone's going to freeze to death out there," he scolded.

Ashton patted him on the shoulder. "As a first act of your new deputyship, I think you should be in charge of crowd control. Good luck." Ashton handed Jimmy the platter and held the back door open.

The women cheered and Jimmy returned his greeting with a huge smile.

Amanda pulled out two cakes from the refrigerator.

Ashton sighed. "I sure am going to miss Victoria's cakes."

Amanda lifted Ashton's chin and looked at him with desire. "I've been making her cakes all week." She lifted up the smaller of the two. "This one is my own twist on her original."

Ashton leaned in and kissed her. She returned his kiss, pressing her body into his. His hands traveled down her neck to the top button of her blouse. Amanda pulled back slightly, leaving Ashton breathless.

"I think we can just leave the large cake for the ladies here on the table," Amanda whispered.

"Jimmy can throw it to them before he padlocks the door behind him," Ashton agreed, leaning in for another kiss.

"Put your coat on," Amanda giggled.

"You know, it's a funny thing," Ashton protested. "The last thing I want to do is put more clothes on at this moment."

"We're taking this party and this cake to your place," Amanda instructed.

"You don't want to stay with the coven?"

"I said my good-byes hours ago. Besides, we need to share a piece of cake together."

"You've decided to give in," Ashton sighed with relief. "Victoria would be proud. Tell me, what does this particular recipe of yours do?"

"Take me to your place and find out."

"Seriously, what does it do?"

"Let's just say you won't be needing a garden or a gun belt for what I have planned."

Chapter 12

Cold Case Clairvoyance 001:
The Belle Isle Lady in White

Blog Post:

Inheritance is both a blessing and a gift. I can't complain. My amazing, strong willed, stubborn, binge-drinking-inspired, reckless, brave, fierce, beautiful, passionate, powerful mother left me her house, her cat and a library full of hidden testimonies to unsolved murders that go back centuries. Sure, I would have preferred stocks and a cabana on Grand Cayman. Instead, she left me the burden of being a voice for the voiceless. She also left all of this inheritance in a town smaller than my former Chicago apartment living room.

Why stay? Why not just sell the place and donate the stories to the historical society and be done with it? It's not that easy. Nothing worth doing ever is.

While I write, the world's sexiest sheriff is fixing my roof. I've been single my entire adult life in Chicago and wouldn't it figure I'd find love in this pasty-with-gravy town. Talk about "looking for love in all the wrong places." In fact, this town, with its pragmatic love of snowmobile boots and wood burning stoves, is the absolute last place I ever would have thought to look for love. Yet here I am, stoking the stove and hoping it's hot enough in here so the sheriff will take off his shirt...and any other articles of clothing he feels unnecessary when he come in for dinner.

I have to say it, Victoria. You win. Like all good mothers, your insistence on the return of the prodigal daughter is my overflow of abundance. I have a house under repair after a run in with a real life urban legend, a love, a purring cat in my lap and I have a new purpose. I have you, dear reader. For all of this, and more, I am grateful. My life, as it turns out is much better than I expected. Sadly, there are thousands of lost souls who could not say the same. They were silenced before their time and their final moments hidden in history. Men, women and most deplorably, children.

If you have ever been seated around a campfire at night in any Michigan town, you will have heard the ghost story of the Lady in White. As a teen, I myself made plans to visit Belle Isle at night. The urban legend suggests that to see her, one must call to her by turning on your car headlights and honking your horn three times.

There is always a little bit of truth in every legend, but do you want to know the true story of this Native American Chief's daughter? The legend says she was so beautiful that the warriors of the tribe could not keep her many suitors away. She was pursued. She was kidnapped. Her father grew so afraid for her safety that he wrapped her in white robes and marooned her on Belle Isle.

That is where her modern story ends. In my latest interview with a secret source, I will reveal the real story filled with pirates, poisonous snakes, an ancient curse and a real life princess waiting for her prince.

To be continued….

And now a sneak preview of Michele and MM's next paranormal mystery!

The Snake Princess

By

Michele Roger

Chapter 1

Jessica could feel his warm breath on the back of her neck as his fingers slowly discovered the buttons of her sweater. It may have been October, but the heat from their two bodies made the lovers impervious to the plummeting, fall temperatures. Amanda turned in the dark and pulled Adam closer until her mouth found his. He kissed her hard. She was eager too. She whispered between kisses, "Did you bring the blanket?"

Adam reluctantly pulled his body from hers to turn and reveal a rolled up sleeping bag from his backpack. "I brought everything. Tonight, is going to be perfect," he assured her. "No parents, no curfew, just you, me, the beach and the moon."

Jessica bit her lip. "Did you remember the condoms?" As soon as she said it, she was grateful for the cover of night. The intensity of her embarrassment immediately tightened her stomach, and she felt a wave of nausea wash over her. Adam surely would have seen it if they had more than the moon and stars to illuminate their faces.

Adam held up two purple packets confidently between his index and middle finger. "Stole them from my brother," he announced proudly.

Jessica crossed one foot over the other, sheepishly. She and Adam had been dating for just shy of four months and had spent the last two weeks planning their secret meeting on Belle Isle. She watched Adam as he smoothed out the blanket and placed the condoms on the corner. He returned to her, taking her in his arms. A nervous shiver ran through her body, and she trembled.

"We'll go slow like we planned," he whispered. "I love you," he added.

"I love you too," she sighed, burying her head in his chest. She felt like she was standing on a cliff, high above a village below. She had left the people and places she'd known that afternoon as a person who had only known herself in all the ways that were intimate and private. In the morning, she knew she would be different. She wasn't sure how exactly, but to offer access to her body in a way no one had ever explored or touched was guaranteed to change her.

For all the shyness that she felt looking at the condom packets, it seemed to melt away the minute they were in each other's arms. She kissed Adam gently, at first. As their lips lingered, the desire grew. Jessica's head swam with a wanting she had never known before. Her heart beat so hard she thought it might burst from her chest. "Ok," she heard Adam whisper in her ear. "Like we planned." Reluctantly, she stopped kissing him but smiled. This was it.

She loved him so much in that moment. He wanted it to be special for her. So many of her friends 'boyfriends had never given any thought at all to their first time. "I'll be right back," she said with a nervous giggle.

She left the soft sand of the beach and stepped over tall sea grass, making her way to the tree line. Her fingers trembled with nerves and cold as she took off her sweater and shimmied off her jeans. She nearly fell over and laughed at herself as she struggled to hurriedly remove her sneakers and socks. She heard the rustling of the brush in the darkness.

"No peeking," she scolded. "Besides, I'm ready." Jessica shivered and returned to the sandy beach where she stood with her arms across her breasts. Her teeth chattered as she called Adam's name.

Saplings just beyond the edge of the moonlight moved. She smiled with relief. Adam stepped into the light and gave her a smoldering smile. He offered his hand to her and she took it. He kissed her as he pulled her to him, and Jessica was grateful for the warmth of his body with hers.

Resisting their nerves and the cold, they ran to the blanket hand in hand and the two fell into each other's arms. Jessica breathed in as Adam kissed her neck. As his lips headed south in her body she gasped, trapping her fingers in his hair. He was nearly to her torso, and she heard him hiss.

Her fingers felt his head jerk upwards. "That's an interesting sound," he laughed.

"What?" Jessica asked breathlessly.

But Adam wasn't listening anymore. She heard the crinkling of plastic and opened her eyes to see Adam kneeling over her. "Ready?"

She smiled and took in a deep breath. She sat up and kissed him. He pressed his lips to hers and their two bodies entwined as their passion rose. She wanted him and pulled his hips into her body. He gave her one last look, and as their eyes met, she said goodbye to her innocence.

Adam's face suddenly contorted, instantly changing from a look of pleasure to one of agony. He gritted his teeth. Jessica gripped his arms, pleading, "what's wrong?"

Instead of answering, Adam screamed. Jessica's heart leapt into her throat as she was suddenly aware of the sand moving under the flannel blanket. She tried to sit up, but she was trapped under Adam's rigid body. It felt as if every muscle in his legs and arms were iron bars, pinning her to the ground as he jerked and cried out. She fought to break free.

Then she felt a searing hot pain in her left foot. She heard her scream join Adam's. Her logical mind struggled to make sense of it. The train of thought blurred as the feeling of something cold and leathery brushed past her arm. She tried to gasp but it was hard to breath. Adam stopped screaming and his muscles were trading in their tension for the sensation of his full, heavy weight on her body.

With all her strength, she rolled his body to the left of her and was met with a chorus of hissing.

Adam's face stared up to the sky, blank. His eyes, opening and turning a milky white like the moon itself. Jessica began to sob but her fear told her to run. She stepped hard on the moving blanket, her clumsy feet feebly attempted to propel her to safety. The searing pain hit her hard again in the calf and then again in the thigh.

The moonlight was becoming blurry, and she felt her body stiffen under the power of the moving, slithering beach. Her kneels collapsed and fell to the ground. Jessica willed herself to blink. The moon was walking towards her. The moon, she thought as struggled to take a breath, was beautiful. The moon was a beautiful girl, not much older than herself. Jessica tried to smile but her muscles had long stopped listening to her brain. The poison was in control.

The girl stood before her as if bathed in a robe of white light. Three fathers graced her head like a crown. Jessica knelt before the princess as she struggled to take in one last breath. The princess waved her hand and the snakes obediently gathered at her feet like dogs.

In Jessica's final exhale, she heard the princess whisper, "There is no room for love here on my island."

The words echoed in the girl's ears and her body fell. Her innocent face plummeted into the sand as her eyes turned the milky white color of the full moon.

About the Authors:

M. M. Genet is the author of the romance series "Agent for the Orchestra," "The Harpist," and the upcoming sequel, "The Detective,". She also writes the "Lady of Keys" erotica romance series.
Additionally, she is published under different pen names for her work in horror, children's literature, non-fiction and Food and Travel.
When she isn't writing or promoting a book, she performs as a harpist.

Michele Roger is a harpist, writer and teacher. She's also a mother and a grandmother. She grew up speaking French with her grandmother as a child and continued on reading and writing in the language, later writing music for children in French.
Michele is the author of "Eternal Kingdom: A Vampire Story," "The Conservatory," several short stories, including "Just Like Dolls," and children's stories "Huggy Muggy Do," and "The Harp and Storm Tamer."
She has also written non-fiction books for adults, including "Contemporary Wedding Ceremonies for the Human Race."